# Hey, Neighbor

Sierra Shipley

# Table of Contents

# Books By Sierra

## The Claiming Her Series
*His Temptation*
*His Disaster*
*His Reward*
*His Challenge*

## The Rose Prairie Series
All books in The Rose Prairie Series are standalone set in the
small town of Rose Prairie.

*All Tangled Up*
*Tied In Nots*
*It Had To Be You*

. . . .

## Interconnected Stand-Alone
*Yes, Captain*

# Chapter One

*Elsie*

What the hell is that man doing?

The motorcycle engine revs yet again, making my apartment windows shake from the loud rumble from the parking lot below.

With a huff, I fling my knitting aside, the needles bouncing softly against the plush, tufted ottoman, and stealthily walk over to the window. The sun set several hours ago and the summer's dark has settled in. Fully aware of the light in my apartment, I carefully pull back the curtain to survey the parking lot and the neighbor who noisily works on his motorcycle. The last thing I need is to be seen spying on him from my window.

Sure enough, he's crouched by his Harley, his hair pulled back into a man bun as he messes with the engine. For two years I've had to put up with this motorcycle-riding mountain of a man with long hair and tattoos that seems to bring home a different woman every night.

I'm not a prude, but there are only so many times that I can hear him tell the same jokes and listen to forced feminine giggles through paper-thin walls.

I'm happy with my life. It's quiet, peaceful...predictable. Sure, it's lonely at times, but I'm fine. Really. *I'm fine.* Who needs a man when I have my knitting anyway?

He revs the engine again and I find myself admiring the flex of his forearms beneath the fluorescent lights of the parking lot. Dark ink covers his skin and I wonder what it would feel like to trace each one with a finger. I might not like the man all that much, but I can admire him from a distance. Even I have to admit that though he's frustrating, he's quite the specimen. A strong jaw speckled with scruff, straight nose, broad shoulders, perfect muscles, and that long hair I find irresistible.

But then the engine roars again and the thought quickly fades.

Most of my life is spent admiring. I have a whole life ahead of me and most of my time is spent watching it all and too scared to reach for it myself. Especially when it comes to men. Oh, I've dated, just not all that successfully. It's easier to be alone than it is to put myself out there.

Besides, I've got everything I need right here in my tiny apartment. Comfortable furniture? Check. Four-legged companion? Check. Multiple forms of entertainment and a work-from-home job? Check and check.

Now if only the bane of my existence would get with my program to keep the peace, that'd be great.

Charlie meows and snakes his way through my legs desperate for the attention I focus on my neighbor. "I know, bud," I say, shutting the curtain and blocking the view below. The orange fluffball meows until I pick him up, and the frantic grab for attention lulls into loud, satisfied purrs. I've had Charlie since he was a tiny little kitten and he loves basking in any sort of affection. "You just need all the lovin', huh?" I ask in my baby voice saved specifically for him. He purrs even louder, making me chuckle. "Spoiled brat."

The windows rattle as my neighbor messes with his motorcycle again and my eyes roll so hard I'm surprised they don't fall out. At least I don't have to hear a woman tonight.

# HEY, NEIGHBOR

Sometimes I don't know what's worse: listening to him and his motorcycle or hearing sensual moans through the walls. I guess it depends on my mood. Tonight though, all I want is some peace and quiet as I knit my scarf.

Fed up with me, Charlie wiggles his way out of my arms landing with a quiet thump on the floor. "Well, fine, be that way," I scoff as he bounds down the hallway to my bedroom.

Sitting back on the couch I continue to knit, the soft scraping of the needles relaxing in between the loud bouts of a motorcycle engine. One of these days I'm going to have to confront him about working on his bike this late. He even dragged me out of bed one night when he unceremoniously decided to wake the whole complex with his constant mechanics. Not that anyone else seems bothered by it.

When I first moved in, I made sure to meet my downstairs neighbor, Mr. Fernsby. He's an adorable older gentleman with a cane and hearing aids, which makes him the ideal downstairs neighbor. I can make any noise I want and it won't bother him one bit—but it also means he's not bothered by the roar of the motorcycle.

Since he's all alone, I make sure to check on him, often stopping by for lunch and a chat, always bringing a sweet treat to share. He might not have a lot of teeth, but he sure has a sweet tooth.

So when Kane moved in two years ago, I did my best to be a good neighbor. The apartment next to me had been empty long before I had moved in a year prior and I had gotten used to enjoying my impromptu home concerts and dance sessions. I had to put those on hold until the afternoons when I knew he was gone. Somehow it's not as fun to dance and sing during the middle of the day. It's far more fun to drink, dance, and sing in the cool comfort of the darkness.

Since we share a landing and walls of our second-story apartments, I thought it best to try to introduce myself.

It took a week for me to work up the courage to knock on his door and even then I was left speechless. He flung the door open in nothing but his boxer briefs with his tattooed rock-hard chest in my face. I basically threw the muffins I made at him, barely managing to mutter, "Hi, I'm Elsie, your neighbor," before I retreated back into my comfort zone. I'm not even sure if I gave him time to introduce himself before I took off. I only know his name because women moan it... often.

Our apartment complex is small consisting of four two-story buildings that house four units each with a central parking lot in the middle. We're the only two upstairs apartments in our unit, having to take the metal and concrete steps along the outside of the building to the small landing to get to our doors. He has to walk past my door every day to get to his apartment and every time, I try to hide so he can't see me.

All my life I've tried to make myself smaller, to avoid pain and heartbreak. Which is why I've closed myself off. You can't be disappointed about anything if you don't have expectations, so I stick to what I know.

There's not really a moment in my childhood that I can pinpoint '*there, this is where it all started*' but sometimes I wish I could.

Maybe it's when Davis, the first boy I thought showed interest in me, broke my heart when he didn't want me after sleeping with me. Or maybe it was the sense of being unwelcome or judged in social events growing up.

# HEY, NEIGHBOR

It's possible everything in my life has led me to shelter myself from everyone. Except for my best friend Kelsey, of course, but she lives across the country.

Yeah, it's a bit depressing, but being a recluse has its upsides. I can finally be the version of myself I always wanted to be within these four walls. No pressure to be or act a certain way. I can be the goofball, potty-mouth, unapologetic Elsie not everyone gets to see.

The longer I work on my knitting, the more the noise from outside fades into the background. It's still there, but I do my best to block it out. So much so that the sound of Kane's boots coming up the stairs surprises me.

He's really an unmistakable figure. He has to be at least six-four and has this bad boy aura about him strengthened by the leather jacket and motorcycle. I mean, there's a reason he's able to bring home a different girl almost every night.

The man's beautiful.

I quickly scan my kitchen window, and sure enough, the curtains are wide open. It always seems to be the window I constantly forget about. It opens directly out to the landing, right where Kane has to walk to his door. With no time to covertly run across the living room and into the kitchen without being seen, I brace myself for embarrassment.

I'm completely dressed down in my pajamas, a matching short and button-up set with little lambs bouncing across the fabric. My large and exposed legs are bent beneath me, my long chestnut hair pulled up in a ponytail with wisps of my bangs sticking up from under my headband brushing the frames of my giant librarian glasses—there's only so much of the day that I can handle my contacts.

There's enough light in here for him to see me clearly through the window if he decides to look in.

Which he does.

I'm sure I look ridiculous when his head turns to look through my window to see me watching him. In an out-of-body experience, I see myself through his point of view.

A plump woman surrounded by plush, vibrant pillows, wearing a frightened expression, her knitting needles poised as the ball of yarn slides off the couch and across the floor. An orange cat comes from wherever he's been hiding to bat at the ball making it unspool even more across the floor. The woman screeches at the cat, throwing herself down on the floor, and reaches for the unwinding ball of yarn as the cat dashes across the room out of fright.

Absolute embarrassment very similar to panic winds its way deep to the center of my stomach. Why, oh why, did he have to look in? I want to hide behind my ottoman and die. Not a very dignified death, but nothing about this scenario has dignity.

Chastising myself for being foolish, I sneak a covert look toward the window. All I can make out of his partially hidden features is a hint of a smile pulling at the corner of his beautiful mouth.

# Chapter Two

*Kane*

Grease is smeared across the back of my hand, a new line to add to the dark streaks of my tattoos. One of the perks of having so many is that it's harder to see the effects of my work.

The hood of the beat-up faded silver car slams shut with a loud bang. This wasn't an easy fix, but I enjoy a challenge. To replace the part, I had to slowly pry apart the many components that make up an engine, replace the damaged piece, and put it together again. Most of the guys would've hated this job, but for me, it was a strategic battle: me against the engine.

And I won.

"Alright, Bill," I call across the shop to my boss with a sense of satisfaction. "This one's ready to go."

He puts his clipboard down on the standing tray and weaves through the garage. "How'd you manage that?" He points to the dated car, placing his hands on his hips. "I'm not sure the whole damn thing is worth the cost of the part you just put in it."

The young woman waiting in the customer area was desperate. She'd gone to several other car shops and all of them told her the exact same thing. But I saw the desperation in her eyes and couldn't say no.

"Nah," I shrug, shoving the greasy rag into the pockets of my rolled-down coveralls. "She needed someone to take a chance on her." He doesn't have to know I'm not talking about the car.

Bill holds his hand out for the keys, opening the door and putting them in the ignition. Right on cue, the engine rolls over, purring like a kitten.

"Well I'll be damned," he whistles. "You're one helluva miracle worker." He shuts the door and tosses the keys back to me. "I take it you'll handle it?" He's referring to the bill, so I nod my head, one of my curls bouncing loose.

By the time I get home, I'm freshly showered from the gym with the girl's number from the shop on my phone. She was cute, but I'm not quite sure I'll use the number she gave me. It's the whole 'don't shit where you eat' kind of thing.

My motorcycle rumbles into the parking lot of my apartment complex and right on cue, the curtains of my next-door neighbor pull back.

It's getting harder and harder to keep a straight face when I catch her spying on me. Sometimes I rev the engine more than I have to just to see what kind of reaction I'll get from her. So for fun, I pull back on the throttle again.

As expected, the blinds fling open even wider, and this time I let out a bark of laughter.

The woman seems to hate me and everything I do. My feelings aren't as strong as hers appear to be. I can't dislike someone I don't know.

But I'll admit, she's getting braver. I'm still waiting for the day she confronts me about the noise I make, but other than that first time, she's never knocked on my door.

She's quiet and mostly keeps to herself. We run into each other from time to time, but she hardly utters a word. Hell, I don't think the woman has even sneaked a peek at me except from her window, mostly keeping her eyes down when we cross paths. Part of me wants to break down whatever wall it is she keeps up around herself.

I know she has friends. Last summer, I passed her and her friend on the step, both women laughing and grinning. I'd never seen her so animated before, never seen her smile, or heard her laugh. Occasionally I hear her talking to someone through the walls, but it's all muffled and distorted.

She's a mystery to me.

One that I want to solve.

My boots clomp against the stairs leading up to our doors and I fight the urge to look through her kitchen window. It's a habit I've created, but I can't help myself.

Elsie has the brightest and most comfortable apartment I've ever seen. The blue velvet couch is constantly piled high with blankets and pillows—so many fucking pillows. Her apartment is an explosion of plants, colors, and textures that my eye is drawn to it every damn time.

I absentmindedly drag a hand against the stubble of my jaw, my eyes sliding over to peek through her window. It sounds pervy, but it's not like that. She's somehow managed to create a home out of this dump that we live in, so different from my sparse apartment right next door.

Elsie's nowhere in sight tonight, possibly hiding out like she tends to do. The lamp next to her couch is on, her cat licking itself next to one of the pillows and a book rests open on the coffee table.

I've only seen the woman outside of the apartment a handful of times. My guess is that she almost never leaves, and I don't blame her. If my apartment looked like that, I'd probably stay there too.

Although our apartments are mirrors of each other, mine lacks that sense of home that hers does. After spending all my time at work, the gym, or messing with my bike, the apartment is a place to crash. There's just enough stuff to keep the ladies from fleeing in terror.

The lock clicks open, the air stale from the long day. I flip on the light switch out of habit and head straight for the fridge to make a sandwich before settling on the couch to play video games.

The leather of the old couch creaks as I reach for the remote but a voice leaking through the walls makes me pause. What *is* that? Curious, I stand and follow the sound of the voice into the bathroom.

No wonder I didn't see my neighbor in her living room, she's busy singing in the shower. If I listen closely, I can just make out the music she's singing to. I'm not exactly sure what the song is but the phrase '*man after midnight*' has me chuckling. I feel like my neighbor has more to her than meets the eye.

Smirking, I shove a bite of sandwich into my mouth and head back into the living room, ready to pick up where I left off.

My neighbor must be feeling herself tonight because I've been hearing her voice through the walls since I got home. Even with my headset on and the sound of my rifle shooting down enemies while I shouted at my team don't drown out her terrible singing.

Two years with barely a peep from her and now she's singing all damn night?

# HEY, NEIGHBOR

"What the fuck are you doing, Kane?" Ash, my best friend, shouts at me through my headset. I was so busy focusing on the concert happening next door that my hands stopped moving the controller.

Shaking my head I focus on the task at hand. "Sorry, man. My neighbor is distracting me." The grenade I launch blows up the silo with a loud boom.

"That quiet hermit chick?" he laughs. "She hardly makes a peep, man. What are you talkin' about?"

"Yeah." The controller clicks at a rapid pace as I give Ash directions for our game. "She's been singing all night."

He mutters something that sounds like 'what the hell' before all talk of the girl next door fades into the background, even if her voice doesn't.

# Chapter Three

*Elsie*

That was invigorating.

For two long years I've had to stop my living room dance parties and over-the-top singing, but last night I decided fuck it. That giant asshole of a man has been disturbing my peace that I felt it was time for a little payback in my own way.

My throat's sore from all of my vocal gymnastics from last night and it's all raspy and ragged. Poor Charlie ran away scared when I said good morning instead of coming for his morning snuggles.

A smug grin slides across my face at the thought of my neighbor having to deal with my noise for once.

*Take that sucker.*

I'm not one hundred percent certain he actually heard me through the wall, but I did my damndest to make sure he did. I placed my speaker right against our shared wall and spent plenty of time jamming out in the bathroom and bedroom.

I got lucky enough that he didn't have a girl over, at least from what I could—or rather couldn't— hear. Thank God. If I had to hear one more night of him in the throes of pleasure with a woman, I'm likely bound to combust from all the sexual frustration coursing through my veins.

It's been... a while since I've had a romantic entanglement. Let's just say there's been a lack of male companionship for... I don't know... a decade? I'm a thirty-year-old woman who hasn't had a boyfriend since I was twenty.

It's time to woman up and get out there.

Which is why I downloaded this stupid dating app. It's about time I start to break free of my shell and explore what the world has to offer. After creating my profile, I spent hours swiping through the men that popped up on the screen. I may have gotten a little overzealous and swipe-happy while belting out songs at the top of my lungs.

I'm not sure anything will come from it though, so I try to put the thought in the back of my mind.

My morning routine runs smoothly, even if my nightly antics made my virtual meeting more difficult than it should've been.

I'm one member of a team of twenty representatives who work remotely. My day-to-day is spent managing the payroll of over a thousand employees in the vastly growing online company. I was lucky enough to get a foot in the door straight out of college and worked my way up. When a remote position became available I jumped on it and haven't looked back.

No more stuffy office for me.

I thought that being able to work anywhere in the world meant expanding my horizons. Traveling to the places I always wanted to see. Doing the crazy things I put in my new dating profile as bucket list items.

All it did was make my apartment my tether.

Kelsey says I need to get out and go live my life, but she's far away from California. The most I get out of the state is for our yearly vacations.

After lunch, I take a brisk walk down to the park that's about a mile away and make my way around the gorgeous lake a couple of times before heading back home. It's something I've had to work up to doing since getting out of the apartment sometimes fills me with anxiety.

It's just a walk around the park, a little exercise, and a chance to get out, but I can't help the way I feel. It seems that no matter how much walking I do, the size of my ass and thighs never change. Oh, well. I've come to terms with the fact that I will always have thick thighs. Recently the phrase '*thick thighs save lives*' runs through my brain quite often. Might as well embrace them.

The summer heat has me sweating so badly that I'm surprised the flowers haven't wilted as I walk past. To say I need a shower is an understatement.

After taking off my shoes, I head straight for the bathroom and turn on the water. My sweaty sports bra gives me a run for my money as I try to pry it over my head. Wet spandex and damp skin make the task of removing it nearly impossible.

"Please come off," I whine in a near panic when the damn thing gets stuck around my elbows. Trapped in an undignified position with my arms pinned to my ears trapped by the wayward bra, I give myself a moment of rest. My chest heaves as I give myself a break before going back into battle. The stupid bangs I cut on a whim flop in my eyes adding to my frustration as I try to wiggle free. Finally, with one giant tug, the thing frees itself and I toss it to the floor completely exhausted from the battle.

Thankfully, the spandex leggings don't put up nearly as hard of a fight and I manage to get them down with minimal effort. Which is a relief because my muscles feel like jello.

Steam rises from the shower and I pull back the curtain, thrusting my hand under the water to check the temperature.

Like most women, I enjoy a nice, hot shower to soothe my nerves, but I don't enjoy the thought of being scalded to death.

Happy with the temperature, I place one foot on the floor. Warm water sprays over my shins before recognition hits. Closing my eyes out of irritation at myself I step back onto the bath mat cursing. "Shit. I do this every fucking time."

This morning while I waited for the meeting to start, I decided to be productive and do something instead of twiddling my thumbs. What better way to be productive than to do some laundry? Which means all my towels are currently in the dryer. Not hanging on the towel rack beside the shower.

At least I remembered *before* getting soaking wet, which is what usually happens when I wash towels.

My eyes trail down my naked body to the pile of sweaty workout gear I managed to pry myself out of. There's no way in hell I'm putting those back on. Even if I thought I could, it wouldn't be worth the battle.

The mess of clothes I barely managed to wrestle off my body taunts me and my nakedness. I'm not the kind of girl who enjoys being naked or walking around naked, even in the comfort of my own home. Never have been, and I doubt I ever will. But my choices right now are slim. There's no way in hell I'm going to shimmy my way back into those sweaty clothes.

I've got no choice but to go naked.

Feeling like an intruder in my own home, I peek around the door of the bathroom on my toes. For some reason, I have to sneak around my own apartment when I'm bare-ass naked. It's not like someone's going to jump out at me and scream "Gotcha!"

Charlie sits on the ottoman and lifts his head blinking slowly at me as if surprised. The look is full of judgment as he issues a soft meow.

"Oh, hush. You're naked all the time, so I don't want to see any judgment from you." He stares at me, unblinking. "Thank God you can't talk," I mumble under my breath and stick my tongue out at him for good measure.

The laundry room is a small closet right off the kitchen with a stacked washer and dryer. Easy access to do my laundry was one of the deciding factors for this apartment. There aren't many options with in-unit washers and dryers, so this was a big deal. It means that I don't have to load up my laundry, lug it down the stairs—where I would inevitably fall since I wouldn't be able to see my feet— and spend hours of my day sitting awkwardly waiting for my clothes to dry.

Charlie meows as I step out of the bathroom and I've had it with his sass. Rounding the corner into the kitchen, I turn and toss double middle fingers at my cat, just to prove who's boss.

Pleased with myself a smirk settles on my face at putting my cat in his place.

Which is exactly what Kane sees through my wide-open kitchen window.

Fuck.

Like deer in headlights, our wide eyes lock, both of us frozen. In utter shock, I'm unable to move. Him? I'm not sure exactly what halts his movements. But I guess it's not every day he sees his neighbor standing naked in her kitchen for no apparent reason.

It's my lucky day, I guess.

I'm trapped in a frozen body, my mind whirring but my limbs refusing to move. I've never been in this position before.

What does someone do when they're caught in a compromising position? Scream? Cry? Cover up? Maybe close the fucking curtain? But I can't do anything but maintain the most awkward eye contact of my life.

For the first time, I notice that his eyes are hazel as they flicker from my face to glance down at my abundant display of skin.

I don't think to cover myself, because that would be the smart thing to do. No, I turn into liquid and melt gracelessly onto the tile floor like a melted popsicle.

Face down on the kitchen floor my brain has the audacity to note that I need to sweep in here. Stealing a quick glance up at the window, Kane can still very much see me, and now he's getting a real show because my ass is in the air as I lay prone on the floor.

"Shit. Fuck. Dammit to hell," I hiss, army crawling to the cabinet directly beneath the window, effectively shielding myself. A little too late, I grab the small hand towel hanging from a drawer handle, hold it to my chest, and cover the nipples he already got an eyeful of.

Charlie glances over at me, his head tilting. "What the fuck just happened?" I whisper hiss at him.

Honestly, I don't blame Kane for freezing—or sneaking a look for that matter. I'd probably do it too if I happened to walk by and see him naked. I'd basically done that already, although that was years ago.

It was probably the last thing he thought he would see today.

Charlie doesn't answer my question but watches me with a tilted head as I try to calm my racing breaths.

After several minutes of hugging my legs on the floor, I risk a glance back up to the window. The afternoon sun floods the apartment, dust motes dancing in its rays, but the window is free and clear of any neighbors.

Clutching the small towel to my chest I close the blinds as quickly as possible before shuffling into the laundry room.

The large towel is still warm as I pull it from the dryer and wrap it around my body grateful for its protective cover. Well, this is certainly one way to remember to take the towels out of the dryer before getting in the shower.

I just hope I never have to see his infuriatingly handsome face again anytime soon.

# Chapter Four

*Kane*

The heels of my motorcycle boots clomp up the stairs, a smirk forming at the thought of Elsie knowing I'm coming.

It's been two weeks since I saw her naked through the window. Which means it's been two weeks of me thinking about what I saw when I looked through that window. And damn do I enjoy thinking about it. Way more than I should've been for a peeping tom.

No, I didn't look through her window thinking, *"Man, I hope I see her naked standing in the middle of her kitchen,"* but I still feel like I need to apologize. It was rude to stare the way I did even though I couldn't look away from all her curves on display.

Stepping onto the landing, I'm surprised to see her standing there.

Not only is she outside, looking like a snack in that damn blue dress, but there's a man currently standing very close to her. They look to be engaged in a conversation, with Elsie doing more listening than talking, nodding along with whatever he's saying.

She looks beautiful. She's always been a pretty girl, even when she decided to cut those quirky bangs. But tonight, with her hair down to the curve of her ass and wearing a baby blue dress under the soft glow of the porch lights? She's absolutely stunning.

Her warm brown eyes widen as she spots me over the mystery man's shoulders, but she continues to politely nod through her conversation.

The landing being only three or four feet wide, I'm completely blocked, stuck standing listening to the man go on about fishing reels.

Really? I didn't peg her going after wilderness guys, but it's her choice.

Elsie continues to glance between me and her date, unsure of what to do, so I help her out.

"Excuse me," I say loudly after clearing my throat. "I need to get by if you don't mind."

Her date looks over his shoulder and mumbles an apology as they move out of my way to let me by.

Part of me knows that she wants privacy, but I can't help myself. I guess I enjoy these small little torments to see her reaction, so I take my time unlocking my door. Not surprisingly, Elsie continues to glance my way.

Her date now stands with his back to the railing as Elsie stands in front of her door, all the while glancing surreptitiously over at me. She looks so cute and entirely uncomfortable with the situation that I can't help the smirk that crosses my face.

The key clicks in the lock and I take one last look at my neighbor. Her eyes dart over to mine, seeming distracted by me, so she's unaware that her date is leaning down to kiss her.

Her eyes widen in shock, quickly darting back to the man in front of her as his lips press against hers. A small, surprised squeak slips out but to her credit, she doesn't flinch or jerk away. She stands stock still until he breaks contact, pulling back with an embarrassed smile when he does.

The poor man has no idea how unwanted that kiss was and I stifle a snort as I walk into my apartment, leaving her to deal with the aftermath of...whatever that was.

• • • •

I'M FRESHLY SHOWERED, grime-free from my day at the shop, and tugging on my leather jacket when there's a knock at my door.

Ash and I are meeting at the bar, so I'm not sure who's standing on the other side.

My keys scrape against the counter as I grab them and head to the door, opening it without bothering to see who's on the other side.

"Hey, neighbor," Elsie mutters, nervously rocking back and forth on her feet. She steps back against the railing as I crowd onto the landing before closing my door and locking it. "I um—," her voice dies down to barely a whisper as I face her. She's still wearing the blue dress from earlier, looking as lovely as before, if not a little more flustered. "Well, I know you saw what happened earlier," she starts.

"You mean when Mr. Outdoorsy kissed you?" Scruff scapes against my palm as I fight a grin at the memory.

Her small hand reaches up to rub a spot on her neck. "Yeah," she breathes. "Look, I need your help."

I'm already shaking my head and heading for the stairs. "Whatever it is, I can help you tomorrow. As you can see, I'm going somewhere."

Her shoes clack at a staccato pace as she tries to catch up with me. "No, not that kind of help."

If she doesn't need help with anything, what *does* she need? Intrigued, I halt my steps and raise an eyebrow, waiting for her to continue.

"Good lord you have big steps," she complains quietly. "What I mean is," she circles her hands in front of her, her eyes dancing away. "You're obviously good on dates."

"What do you mean 'obviously'?" I ask, crossing my arms across my chest, the leather groaning from my movement. Color inches up her cheeks, a bright shade of red that I find adorable and do my best to hide my grin.

"The walls are thin," she admits, barely a whisper.

I can't help it. Something about her guilty expression has me tossing my head back with laughter. The walls *are* thin. I knew that's where she was going, I just wanted to hear her say it.

"Shut up," she chides, her voice lightening as she holds back laughter of her own. I guess I'm rubbing off on her already. "I need someone to help me with dating. After what you saw today, I clearly need help, and I think you're the man for the job. The only person I know that can help me," she clarifies.

"Yeah, that was pretty awful."

"It was."

I look up at the night sky and think about what she's asking. She's going out on a limb to ask me to do this for her. All I know is that she's quiet and keeps to herself—aside from being a sneak who likes to hate me through her blinds. But my heart tugs at how vulnerable she's being and I sigh, knowing damn well I'm going to help her.

But she doesn't know that.

Mind already made up, I choose to torment her for just a moment longer. My hand scrapes under my chin and I hum pretending to contemplate my answer.

"You won't have to do anything you don't want to," she rushes, trying to sway me. "I just need some help in getting out of my comfort zone. Talking to people, that sort of thing."

Her brown eyes plead with me and I already know I'm a goner.

"Alright then. Let's go."

"Go? You'll help me?"

"If we're going to do this, I need to see you in action first. What better time to start than the present, and seeing as I'm already going to a bar..." I let my words die off and gesture down the steps.

She crosses her arms and looks back towards her apartment. "I don't know—"

"Else, you asked for my help, and I'm helping you. You need out of your zone? Great. Then let's go." The nickname slips right off my tongue without me even thinking of it. She doesn't seem to mind my shortened version of her name, though.

She huffs a sigh. "Fine. Let me lock up first." I wait as she quietly opens her door, grabbing whatever she needs before pulling it shut and locking it.

"We can take my car," she offers when we reach the parking lot.

"No need," I reply, holding my keys out. "I've got the bike." She pauses in the middle of the parking lot, her eyes locked onto my motorcycle. I hold out the helmet for her, beckoning her closer.

She glances between me, my bike, and her car. "I'm not riding on that thing. You're basically a stranger. For all I know you're going to drag me off into the woods or something."

"Seriously?" I huff, amused. "I've lived next to you for years. You just asked me for dating help because of what you hear through the walls." She looks down embarrassed but I keep going. "Did they sound like they were being murdered to you?"

Elsie taps her heels against the concrete, that lovely shade of red flushing her skin under the lights. "I'm not going to answer that."

God, it's fun to watch her squirm.

"Come on, Else." I offer the helmet again and give her a charming smile. "What am I gonna do? Follow you home?" That earns a huff of laughter and a quiet smile. "What happened to the whole 'getting out of your zone' thing?"

I got her there and she knows it.

We stand at an impasse and I wait patiently for her to see that I'm right. The woman was clear in what she wanted but now she has to follow through with my suggestions.

She looks at the motorcycle again, her face falling. "I've never ridden a bike before," she says timidly. "I don't know what to do."

The pavement grinds under my boots as I cross over to her. She looks up at me through her lashes, her brown eyes wide. "It's easy," I explain wiping her hair away from her face and sliding on the helmet. "Hold on tight and I'll do the work."

The buckle clicks under her chin and I tighten it until it's snug against her head. "Just like sex."

Those cheeks of hers blush under the fluorescent lights, her eyes darting everywhere but at me. "Alright," she sighs. "Anything else I need to know before climbing onto this death trap?"

I throw my leg over my bike with a chuckle and straighten the handlebars before kicking up the kickstand. "Lean into the turn and not against it. And if I go too fast, just tap my shoulder. Now," I pat the empty seat behind me. "Climb on."

She takes a deep breath, eyeing my bike like it's going to bite her before a determined look crosses her face. It takes her a minute to figure out how to climb on without her dress getting in the way, but she manages.

"Put your feet here," I point to the pegs on the side. "If you don't, you'll burn the shit out of your leg." She leans over, holding onto my shoulder to see, her foot missing the mark. "Here," I slide my hand around the smooth skin of her calf and lift her foot onto the peg.

"Thanks," she breathes, as she places her other foot on the peg and wraps her arms around my shoulders.

The motorcycle starts with a roar, the powerful engine rumbling underneath us. Her thighs squeeze tighter against me, her hands in a death grip on my shoulders.

This won't do.

Reaching up, I unhook her hands and wrap them around my chest. "I said to hold on tight," I yell, just before taking off out of the parking lot, making her yelp in surprise.

• • • •

WE'VE BEEN AT THE BAR for an hour before Elsie gets up to use the restroom. Elsie weaves her way through the crowd and is out of earshot as Ash leans across the table.

"What the hell, man? Why is the crazy neighbor here?" Ash has been giving me odd looks all night, but we haven't had a chance to talk about it.

Elsie doesn't seem like the kind of person who wants her business out for everyone to know about, so I won't share our agreement. The only people that need to know are me and her. So I shrug my shoulders and pull back a mouthful of beer.

"Have you lost your damn mind? She's your *neighbor*."

"Maybe."

This whole situation could be a huge fucking mess, but I can't *not* help someone when they need it. I'm a fucking sucker and I know it. And shit, does she need some help. The woman has been a shaking ball of anxiety the moment she got off the bike, though admittedly that's mostly my fault. The opportunity was there for the taking, so I took it.

After peeling out of the parking lot with a screaming Elsie, I did a little dodging and weaving between cars for a few minutes before taking pity on her. When we got to the first red light, her small hand smacked the back of my head. It didn't hurt, but it made me laugh.

"What happened to 'don't shit where you eat'?"

"It's one night out, Ash. There is no shitting. Or eating," I add with a wink.

"It's official, you've lost it. You've finally lost it," he says, tossing back the last of his drink and immediately setting off for the bar to order more.

He's not wrong, maybe I have lost it. Lost it because even though she's a hermit, there's something about her that feels like home. Sure, she's awkward as hell and has been shaking like a leaf all night, but there's potential there.

I watch as Elsie hunches her shoulders in, her arms folded against her chest as she maneuvers through the bustling crowd to our table.

It's like this woman has no confidence in herself. Not just right now, I noticed when she met Ash that her eyes constantly looked to the floor and that she barely said two words to him before we sat down.

This shy, hermit of a woman needs a confidence boost.

Ash rolls his eyes as I stand and grab my beer. "Have fun, Ash."

He issues a quiet "fuck you" as I meet Elsie in the middle of the floor.

"I have an idea." I place my arm around her shoulders, her body tucked against my chest as I lead her to the bar.

"What are you doing?" She looks up at me with furrowed eyebrows.

"Well, Else, we're going to do a little experiment." I grab the bartender's attention and motion for another drink for my neighbor. Having a drink in her hand might help to keep her distracted from what I'm going to make her do.

She places her hands on the polished wood bar palms down as if to brace herself. "Oh, God. Do I want to know?"

"Probably not." She rolls her eyes at my wide smile and I laugh at her. The bartender sets her beer in front of her and she takes it whispering, "I've made a terrible mistake," before taking a long drink.

"I want to introduce you to some people." I lead her over to a group of guys who sit chatting at a table.

For such a timid girl, she puts up a fight as we get closer to the table. With every step she digs her heels into the floor, pushing against me. She's a feisty one, I'll give her that.

A chorus of introductions is made and I carefully watch the woman standing next to me as she clutches her drink with both hands, her smile tight. These are nice guys and they try to include her in the conversation, asking her questions, but she answers them quickly before letting her voice fade into the background, more than happy to let the conversation continue without her.

She's polite but lacks the animation and personality that I'm starting to get glimpses of. I knew she was shy, but I figured she'd warm up the longer we spent talking, but no.

Elsie downs her entire drink as we stand there talking, her fingers tapping against the glass. Chris offers to buy her another drink, but she simply shakes her head issuing a polite no thank you before glancing down to the floor.

It seems that my neighbor needs a confidence boost.

I know exactly where to start.

# Chapter Five

*Elsie*

Thank God tonight's coming to an end.

This whole night has been a whirlwind which I guess was the whole point. First, I never go to bars, let alone one as busy as this one. And I especially don't make a habit of approaching a table full of attractive men who wouldn't look twice at me.

It's clear that this place is Ash and Kane's regular prowling spot full of beautiful women who scream 'Take me home with you.'

I'm surprised that I wasn't ditched by the number of women who showed interest in them when I was sitting right next to them. It was almost like I was invisible to them. Not a threat.

Hell, I am invisible.

Kane, thankfully, has slowed down his driving and isn't trying to purposefully scare the shit out of me anymore at least. I know exactly what he was doing earlier, the asshole. After the first shock of being on the back of a motorcycle as it zoomed through traffic, I have to admit that it was pretty damn fun. I can see why he enjoys it so much.

The bike bounces over the uneven pavement into our parking lot and I squeeze myself tighter against his strong back to keep from falling off. It's nice to feel his strength under my hands. After all, it's not every day that I get to wrap myself around a handsome hunk of a man with a too-charming smile even if I hate him.

God, he's almost too good-looking.

His brown wavy hair blows into my face, his cologne right along with it. A combination of bourbon, mahogany, and something rugged that has me fighting the urge to bury my nose in his neck. I tell myself the deep inhale and the way my eyes slip closed as I breathe him in is a reflex.

Kane pulls into his assigned parking spot, right next to my sensible compact car, cutting the engine and setting down the kickstand.

The rumbling vibrations of the engine beneath me have my legs feeling like jello and he laughs as he helps me off the bike. Kane's large hand grips mine, keeping me from crumbling to my knees.

"So, how was your first experience on a bike?" He reaches up and unclips the helmet under my chin, and the way his eyes sparkle down at me has me feeling some sort of way and I quickly look away. Heat blooms where his skin touches mine making it hard to concentrate.

I fiddle with my fingers as he pulls the helmet off my head. "It wasn't as bad as I thought it would be. Once you got scaring me out of your system," I add spitefully.

He follows after me through the parking lot, his voice tinged with warmth. "You gotta live a little, Else. There's no fun without livin' on the edge."

"Why do you think I'm doing this?" I mumble under my breath as I trudge up the steps, Kane hot on my heels.

"Well," I say a little louder, stopping in front of my apartment door, "thanks for agreeing to help me. Now you can see what my issues are," I add with a sigh.

This whole thing is an act of desperation. George had been nice enough, but Kane was right. He's not my type. The whole date he talked about fishing, kayaking, hiking... all things that I will probably *never* be comfortable with.

And that kiss? Ugh, it was terrible. It's not like I was sending George '*kiss me*' signals. I was trying to be polite.

It didn't help that Kane was standing there, watching as I tried and failed to bail on the date. I couldn't stop myself from looking over at his smug face and that smirk that made his eyes crinkle in the corners. Then, he laughed when George kissed me. He tried to hide it, but I heard it.

Once Kane went inside, I quickly and politely thanked George for our date and ran inside, fuming at my neighbor who could have any girl he wanted.

Then I got to thinking about needing a teacher or coach—someone who could tell me what to do and when to do it. And of course, Kane's face popped into my head.

I'm kind of regretting my decision right now.

"Oh, I know where to start alright," he drawls.

*Great*, I think rolling my eyes and shoving my key into the lock.

"You know," he says, stopping me. "You're an attractive woman. You look amazing in that dress."

The urge to dismiss him is hard to fight, but I turn to where he's casually leaning against the railing.

"Well, thank you." I grit my teeth to keep from saying more and reach for the knob.

Kane's hand caresses my shoulder. "Wait, Else."

35

Begrudgingly I turn towards him ready for this day to be over. His hands cup my face, forcing my gaze to his. I couldn't look away from him even if I wanted to.

"You're a beautiful woman. Any man should consider himself lucky to be seen with you." His thumb strokes over my jaw, the movement sweet and tender. "I'll keep telling you until you believe it."

Where is all of this coming from? We've gone from being barely acquaintances to this, him telling me how beautiful I am. Every ounce of logic tells me that he's spouting pretty words like he does with any girl. He doesn't have to. We're not anything and will never be anything other than cordial neighbors. Granted not every neighbor helps the other with their dating life but there's something in his words that's tinged with something different.

Something that rings true.

I should push him away, get some distance between his tender words and even more tender touch. One simple thing keeps me rooted in place: a man's never looked at me the way Kane's looking at me now. It's the look on every lead man's face from a romance movie when he spots the heroine. His hazel eyes are soft, his voice low and smooth.

I suck in a breath as the words sink in, tears beginning to well up in my eyes.

No one's called me beautiful before.

Kane strokes my jaw one more time and leans down, placing his lips against mine.

This kiss is nothing like my last. It's unexpected, but that's the only thing they have in common. Kane knows exactly what to do, hugging my body to his, a hand cradling my head tenderly as he works his magic.

It takes me a minute to comprehend what's happening, but Kane doesn't relent or move his mouth from mine until I start to kiss him back. I'm still entirely in my head shocked that my neighbor whom I have disliked for years is kissing me.

Kissing the hell out of me.

He slides his hand through my long hair, angling my mouth higher, his teeth nipping at my bottom lip. My hands grip his forearms pulling me closer to him and I let myself fall into whatever he's offering, as I kiss him back.

He makes a sound of shock as my teeth playfully pull at his lower lip, and when his tongue slides into my mouth, I'm the one moaning.

Kane knows exactly what he's doing. Knows which buttons to push, which moves to make. He's forcing me to take in his words, showing me with his mouth, teaching me that I am wanted and desired.

After a second or an eternity, he breaks the kiss, our mouths separating like honey dripping from the comb, slow and smooth.

"Good night, Else."

Dazed from the kiss and a touch tipsy from all the beer I drank, I stand in my doorway stunned as Kane gives a cocky grin and slips inside his apartment.

What the hell have I gotten myself into?

• • • •

KANE'S HOME. THE SOUND of his motorcycle as he pulls into the parking lot is unmistakable.

For days, I've holed myself in my apartment even more than usual. I've gone so far as to close all the curtains and live in the dark like a vampire.

Charlie's been giving me the evil eye, but I stick my tongue out at him whenever he complains, which is often. But he doesn't know about the drama that's brewing with the neighbor next door.

Drama that my idiot self brought on.

In five hours, I went from not being kissed in a decade, to being kissed twice in the same day. By *two* different guys.

Who the hell am I?

After that mouthwatering kiss, I don't think I can face Kane again. It was a pity kiss and that makes me feel terrible about it. I didn't want his pity, but it's what I got. There's no way that a man like him would kiss a girl like me unless he feels sorry for me.

Which is why I'm hiding.

As per usual, he revs his engine a handful of times before finally calling it a night.

The book that I'm nose-deep in is finally getting to the reverse harem part of a reverse harem and his interruption is entirely unwarranted. I may be a sexually frustrated hermit and these books are my lifeline. Him being an ass isn't going to stop me from enjoying my book.

Heavy boots clomp up the stairs even louder than normal, the whole floor shaking with each step. Is he doing it on purpose to annoy me? It's starting to feel like it. He's not clomping, he's practically jumping up each step by the way the whole building rattles.

Does he have a woman with him? Is tonight one of those nights that I have to hear him through the walls? The thought is painful.

The urge to wander over to the window and take a peek is almost unbearable, but I manage it. I sigh in relief as I hear the muffled click of his door closing.

Crisis averted.

Nerves finally settled, I adjust my blanket over my lap and sink deeper into the couch. Now where were we...

*"The four men,* my *four men, surround me, each one gloriously naked. It doesn't matter that they are mafia men who kill with their bare hands, they are* mine.

*Max pulls my lips to his as Thomas runs his hand down my spine, reaching around to cup my breast. Zane leans back in his chair, his cock in his hand while Dom kneels in front of me looking up with a mischievous glint in his eye before his tongue—"*

A loud, brutal knock on my door sends the book flying across the room. Charlie jumps up quick as lightning to dodge the wayward paperback, barely escaping its path of destruction to run and hide.

Another loud pound lands on the door. "C'mon, Else. I know you're in there."

*Shit.*

I scramble off the couch, panicking. Anxiety spreads through my chest knowing there's no way to avoid him. He knows I'm here, and as much as I'd like to think so, he's not an idiot.

"Open up, Elsie, or I'll kick the door down."

*What the fuck?*

I look down at my bare legs, my sweatshirt barely falling to mid-thigh, and race into my room to find some damn pants.

"Alright, Else," he yells through the door, "you've given me no choice. Three, two…"

I pause mid-step, my eyes pinballing between my bedroom where pants are waiting, to the front door about to be kicked down by my giant of a neighbor.

"Wait!" I yell jogging over to the door swiftly unlocking it and pulling it open fully expecting to see Kane braced for impact.

Except that he's not.

He looks like every girl's dream book boyfriend casually leaning against the door jam, his wavy hair falling to his chin, his arms crossed in a mouthwatering pose. That infuriating smirk of his settles across his delicious mouth, his hazel eyes running down my body making me shiver.

"There she is," he drawls, kicking himself off the wall and walking past me into my apartment, completely unfazed at my homeless appearance.

"Please, do come in," I mutter to the now-empty space in front of my door before slamming it shut.

He stands in the middle of my apartment, his head swiveling as he surveys my sanctuary.

For some reason, I feel anxious as he looks at my home. It's my space and having him in it is like opening up my brain and letting him wander through it. There's nothing to hide or cover up within these four walls. All my interests and passions are laid bare because the only person who gets to see them all displayed are me and Kelsey when she visits.

I've spent years carefully selecting pieces that make it feel cozy, from the plush furniture, the soft rugs, mountains of throw pillows, candles of all different scents, lamps with adjustable lighting, blankets on the back of the couch and hanging from the blanket ladder, and my many plants.

He turns in a circle looking too large in my small living room. "You've been dodging me," he accuses.

"No, I haven't," I lie, crossing my arms defensively. "I don't know what you're talking about."

"Sure," he snorts, walking over to my closed curtains, prying them open, and looking through the blinds.

I watch him carefully as he slides the curtains closed, then looks around the room, his eyes catching on the floor behind me.

"What's this?" he asks, sliding past me to pick something up off the floor. "*My Four Mafia Men?*" Kane flips through pages, his eyes widening at whatever he finds there. "Is this a dirty book?" he asks, voice laced with mock shock.

"No," I squeal, reaching for it before he can read anymore. He holds the book high above his head, well over where my five-foot-four frame can reach. "Give it back," I grit out, standing on my tip-toes and using his shoulders for leverage, not caring that doing so exposes my ass.

"The quiet girl next door reads smut...That's sexy, Else. I like it."

His scruff brushes against my cheek as I try and fail to grab my romance novel out of his large hands. His chin dips lower until our mouths are inches apart, and I break. Swirls of anxious anticipation twine in my stomach at how near he is.

Flashes of what that mouth felt like against mine have my heart rate increasing with each breath.

"Fine," I huff, stepping away from him and plopping on the couch. "Why are you here?"

He lowers the book, his eyes glued to the pages, apparently having found a spicy scene. "You've been avoiding me," he mutters distractedly. "We made a deal and I plan to follow through with it."

Which is precisely why I'm avoiding you.

"Were you reading this when I knocked on the door?" he asks, eyebrows raised.

I sigh, grabbing my blanket and throwing it over my lap to cover my deflated thighs. "If you must know, yes. I was. It was getting quite interesting before you ruined the mood." There's no point in lying to him about it. I was caught with the evidence on the floor.

"Ruined the mood, huh?" He quirks a grin, letting the book fall onto the ottoman, and sits next to me on the couch. "Damn, this thing is comfortable." He tosses a pillow behind his head, sighing as he relaxes into it. "What part were you at?"

I'm not sure if he ruined the mood or if he's walked in like a scene from one of my spicy books. Being close to him, with my body humming with arousal, is making it difficult to focus on anything other than the stretch of his shirt over his chest or how his hand rests on his stomach as he settles into the couch.

Something about Kane makes me feel less self-conscious about, well, everything. Plus, there's no point in hiding what I've been reading since he caught me red-handed.

"It was a group scene," I explain, trying to not be embarrassed about my reading habits. "I've been waiting the whole book for it, and you had to interrupt me."

"Group scene, huh? Wouldn't have pegged you for that." His eyes slide closed as he lounges unwelcome on my couch.

Something tells me that my dreams tonight will start with Kane like this and end with us panting and sweaty all thanks to my overheated libido.

"I'm not," I say a tad too defensively.

His eyes slide over to me, his eyebrow arched. "Don't be afraid of what you want, Else. You want three mafia men, you could have them."

"Four," I correct, leaning my head back. "It was four mafia men. And I'm always afraid, that's why I need you," I add.

"We'll just keep on doing what we did the other night," he says as if it's no big deal. "Eventually you'll have enough confidence to continue a conversation. There's no need to be scared. They're just guys."

I want to point out our vast differences but I don't. He doesn't know what it's like to grow up a girl and experience the harsh critiques of others about your body. He never had to suffer that look that crosses men's faces when they dismiss you with a glance. How their eyes slide over my body before looking me in the eyes with nothing but rejection. There's no point in trying to continue a conversation after that. They've already made up their minds and no amount of talking will change that.

I suck in a deep breath hoping to ease the sting of my thoughts. "That's easy for you to say. You're not scared of anything. I bet you could find your perfect woman without lifting a finger." A long, sexy finger attached to an equally sexy man. Yeah, he could probably lock eyes with her and she'd melt and I wouldn't blame her.

Kane smirks, his eyes sliding open to look at me. "I'm going to have to try that."

"Great, all I did was add to your ego."

He laughs easily. It's strange to be sitting here so close to him and not feel like I'm doing everything wrong. "Thanks, Else. I'm flattered. But I have a feeling you could do the same."

"Pft, yeah right," I brush him off. "I'd be too scared to even approach a guy I want, let alone point a finger at him and beckon him closer." The mental image has me cringing.

"Alright," he sits up, clapping. If Charlie hasn't hidden, he sure has now. "Time to face your fears." Kane pats my blanket-covered lap as I eye him wearily. "You're going to tell me what you want. Maybe I could find him for you."

# Chapter Six

"**N**o. Absolutely not." She says it with more force than I thought she had.

"Else, how am I supposed to help you if I don't know what you want? You've gotta give me something to work with here. I'm sure I can think of a dozen guys who'll match what you're looking for."

If I'm honest with myself, I came over here without a plan. All I know is that my cranky neighbor who loves spying on me through her blinds has been radio silent since I kissed her, and I can't have that. Not when that was the best and most surprising kiss I've had in quite some time. There's something about kissing a woman who hates me and feeling her melt beneath my touch that's left me wanting more.

More of Elsie.

"I'm not going to share that with you," she scoffs. "It's embarrassing."

I give her a stern look, turning myself on the couch to face her. "More embarrassing than being caught reading a sex book?"

We stare off for a minute until she throws her hands up in defeat.

"Fine."

"See," I say smiling, "that wasn't so hard, was it?" The death glare in those brown eyes has me laughing. She's shy and timid but can be feisty as hell.

"I hate you."

"Oh, I know." I give her my biggest smile knowing it will annoy her. "Now, what do you want?"

"How specific do you want me to be?" She huddles deeper into the couch, her head resting on the armrest.

I know that all of this is hard for her. It's easy to see that she's got a wall up, but we've got to break through it. She may have asked for my help, and she has it, but she's gotta give me something to work with.

"We'll start slow and work our way up. First, tell me what type of guy you're looking for. Whatever app you're using isn't doing you any favors if that guy the other night came from it."

The image of him leaning in and kissing Elsie when she wasn't paying attention flashes in my mind. She deserves better than that.

"Okay," she sighs, reaching for a pillow and holding it to her chest as she thinks. "I want someone who can pull me out of myself. I need someone who can get me to do the things I want to do, but I'm too scared to do them. Someone who can look at me and know what I'm thinking without having to say a word. I need someone fun, outgoing—a bit of a goofball, ya know? But isn't scared to be serious. A man with a good heart too. Someone who cares for others just as much as he cares for himself." She glances over at me. "That what you wanted?"

If she wants an imaginary man brought to life, then I'll try my damndest to find him.

"Sure, Else." I reach over and pat her knee, the soft fabric of the blanket warmed against her skin. "Now on to the good stuff."

She sits up, her blanket slipping and exposing her bare thigh. For a moment all I can think about is touching that silky smooth skin, what it would feel like under my rough hands.

"What do you mean, 'good stuff'?" She uses her fingers as air quotes, her eyes narrowing at me.

A mischievous grin settles on my face at the thought of how she'll respond. I can't help myself. I enjoy seeing her flustered and snarky.

"What do you like sexually?"

Elsie shoots off the couch like a rocket, her pillows and blanket tumbling to the floor. I choke down my laughter, my eyes glued to her thighs as she stomps across the room.

"And we're done here," she says, opening the door and indicating I walk through it.

I ignore her, picking her dirty book off the coffee table where I left it. "Should I just go through the book scene by scene and see what reaction I get?"

She eyes me wearily as I flip through the pages looking for a smut scene. If this is a dare, I'm not backing down.

"Oh, here we go." I clear my throat and start reading. "Max has my legs thrown over his shoulders, my wet pussy ripe for devouring. He takes a long, leisurely lick from my opening to my clit making my back arch." The sound of the door slamming makes me smile, but I keep reading. "The mattress dips as Dom settles next to me, his head lowering to take my nipple in his mouth—"

The book is ripped out of my hands and lands with a thump on the floor. "That's enough," she hisses, her face turning a lovely shade of pink.

"Did that get you all worked up, Else?" I tease. "Everyone loves a good pussy eating."

She stands in front of me shifting her weight between her feet. Her arms are crossed under her chest and she's looking anywhere but at me. Something about how she's reacting sends warning bells through my mind.

"Wait," I stammer, rising to my feet. "You've had your pussy licked before, right? Jesus, don't tell me you're a virgin."

"I'm not a virgin," she blurts but doesn't say anything more.

"Thank God for that. But that's not all I asked."

She hugs herself tighter, her pink cheeks turning red. "Not that it's any of your business, but no, I haven't."

How could she possibly have gone through life without being eaten out? Hell, it's one of my favorite pastimes, if not my favorite thing of all time. "How the fuck does that happen?" A form of anger I'm unaccustomed to boils over.

"I don't know. It just... never happened."

What a goddamn shame.

"Okay then." I stand and remove my jacket before tossing it on the coffee table. "Let's do this." Her eyes widen as I lift my shirt over my head and let it fall to the floor.

Elsie swallows, her breathing shallow. "What are you doing?" Her voice is quiet, but her eyes slide over the tattoos on my chest.

I take slow steps to where she stands, arms still crossed making the hem of her sweatshirt rise to expose more of that delicious skin.

"First," I say, reaching up to cup her face, "we're going to get you out of this." I crook a finger under the neck of her top.

"Then, you're going to sit on that couch and let me show you what you've been missing. You okay with that, Else?"

Her brown eyes meet mine. "Why would you—" but I don't let her question anything as I bring my mouth to hers.

She's everything that I've been craving.

Elsie melts against me, her soft moans urging me on. Her arms, once folded against her chest, loosen, her small hands cold against my chest as she leans into me. Her lips are soft, warm, and oh-so delicious.

It makes me want her more.

Our lips part slowly. "I do it because I want to. I like the feeling of you pressed against my lips, and I'm sure I'll like the taste of your pussy even more. A beautiful woman like you deserves to be worshiped."

Her breath shudders as I inch my hand under the hem of her sweatshirt, grabbing a handful of her luscious ass. She's got a great ass with more to hold onto, and I love it. I kiss her again, her tongue dancing with mine.

Elsie doesn't protest as I gently lead her to the couch until we're standing right in front of it.

"You okay with this, Else?" Even though I want to do this for her, I don't want to push her. This wasn't part of our agreement and I'm pushing outside the boundaries.

Her breasts brush against my chest with each heavy breath. "Y-yes."

Thank fuck.

"Good," I breathe. "Now let me take care of you." In one swift motion, her sweatshirt falls to the floor leaving her in nothing but her underwear and socks.

I've seen her naked before by accident, but this is different. Last time we were both surprised. This time we're willing participants.

Elsie sucks in a ragged breath, her hands moving to cover her breasts, but I stop her. "Don't cover yourself from me, Else." My finger slides under her chin, tilting her head to meet my gaze. "I want to see you. Look at you. Remember what I said. You're beautiful. There's nothing to hide." Leaning down, I kiss her lips lightly.

"O-okay." She nods her head, her hands slowly falling away.

She's all softness and curves. Her breasts are small, but mouthwatering and I can't wait to suck on the tight nipples beading under my gaze. Her waist flares out to luscious hips and shapely thighs.

She's a feast for the eyes and I can't wait to devour her.

"The polka-dot panties are a nice touch," I tease as my lips brush against her neck.

"Shut up," she chastises, but her hands settle on my back as I kiss my way down her collarbones. My teeth graze against her soft skin and she sucks in a breath.

"Time to take these off."

I hook my fingers into the elastic of her underwear and slowly sink to my knees, dragging them down with me. She shivers, either from nerves or anticipation, but I kiss her luscious thigh in reassurance before standing, dragging my hand over her round hip, and to her breasts.

"What," she swallows nervously, "what should I do?"

God, this woman's trust in me is breathtaking. To have never had someone take the time for her, to do this thing for her, infuriates me.

# HEY, NEIGHBOR

I glide my thumb over her nipples teasing them into points. "You call the shots." I place a kiss on her mouth before pulling back. "I'd like for you to sit on the couch and spread those legs for me. Only if you want to," I reassure her.

She nods her head, then lowers herself onto the couch.

Sinking down between the coffee table and her knees I trail my hands down her calves pulling off the fuzzy socks from her feet and tossing them to the side. Her brown eyes watch me as I lean over to take a nipple into my mouth.

A gasp explodes from her, her hands sinking into my hair, holding me close. I can feel her body shaking underneath me, feel the rise and fall of her chest against me, urging me on. I release her nipple with a pop and look up at her face. Her cheeks are flushed, her eyes shut tight, and her lips parted. She looks so sexy like this and I can't wait to feel her cunt fluttering against my mouth.

I settle my hands on her hips kissing my way down the swells of her belly. Her muscles tense with my exploration and I pause. I don't want her stuck in her head thinking about anything other than pleasure. "You are so beautiful," I whisper against her skin between kisses. I repeat it until the stiffness in her body fades away as I place kisses along every curve of her skin.

"Lean back for me." My voice is unrecognizable to my ears, rough and deep with lust for my neighbor who does as she's told. She parts her thighs beautifully for me. "Good girl," I praise again. "Just like that." I kiss the inside of her left thigh, then her right, slowly inching my way up to the juncture of her thighs.

"You don't have to do this," she stammers.

Her words stop in my tracks, and I flick my eyes up her body. Her arms are crossed over her eyes like she's embarrassed or forcing me to do this.

"Elsie," I say with more force than I intend and wait until her arms fall away and those chocolate-brown eyes meet mine. "If you think there's anywhere else I'd rather be right now, you're wrong. Only you and God can keep me from burying myself between your legs. Understood?"

To prove my point, I lower my head between her spread legs and lick.

Elsie sucks in a breath but I'm lost in the taste of her. She tastes like honey on my lips and my chest rumbles with satisfaction. I take my time reveling in every pant, every moan that escapes her lips.

"You taste fucking delicious, Else."

My cock is rock-hard in my jeans, but I ignore it. This is all about her.

Elsie writhes beneath me, her breath hitching as my tongue swirls over her clit, first softly, then applying more pressure.

"Kane," she whimpers, her legs beginning to tremble. "It feels so good."

Her hands slide into my hair, tugging lightly and I'm filled with pride at the confidence she's exuding. She's lost in the pleasure, her hips rolling with each brush of my tongue. I reach up and toy with her nipple and she shudders with her brewing orgasm.

Pride swells in my chest at how well she's doing. How perfect she is.

I explore her folds before focusing my attention on that bundle of nerves. Elsie writhes under my ministrations, her breathless whimpers growing louder with each swipe of my tongue and I know she's close to coming.

"Yes, Kane. Fuck, yes," she moans. "Don't stop."

Her hips have lost all rhythm, her movements becoming frenzied the closer she gets to orgasm. With one last swirl, Elsie shudders, her body bowing on the couch as her orgasm barrels through her.

Lost in the thrill of Elsie coming on my tongue I continue to work her clit as her body pulses. When her body calms its spasms, I kiss my way up her body.

"That was...unbelievable." Her hands slide lazily up and down my spine, her eyes sliding open and trailing down my body. "You—" she pauses, noticing my erection. Her eyes lock with mine as one hand slides down my back and dips into my jeans wrapping around my cock.

"Else—" I catch the hand reaching for my cock. I want her, badly, but this wasn't about me getting what I wanted. I don't want to use her.

Hurt flashes in her eyes and it kills me to be the one who put it there. I kiss her palm gently, hoping like hell it eases the sting.

By the time I leave, I can't help but feel like I'm opening up a can of worms because there's more to my neighbor than meets the eye.

And I'm dying to uncover it.

# SIERRA SHIPLEY

# Chapter Seven

*Elsie*

The scrapes across my palm thrum with pain and sting like hell. At least the cut on my knee seems to be mostly numb even if it's bleeding like crazy. It still hurts, but it's nothing compared to the split skin of my hands.

"This is just fucking perfect."

My walk today hasn't turned out how I imagined it would, which seems to be what my life now consists of—full of unexpected events. How was I supposed to know that my foot would catch on the uneven pavement that's been there for as long as I can remember?

Or, even better, how was I supposed to know that the neighbor I loathe and dragged into helping me, would decide he needed to go down on me?

Nothing could've prepared me for that.

I brush off tiny pebbles and dirt grumbling to myself. "No. No. We are *not* thinking about that."

Carefully, I pick the tiny pieces of gravel embedded in my knee and toss them aside. I guess it could be worse. Someone could've seen me go down which would have been even more embarrassing.

Still, with no other option but to keep moving, I test my weight on my injured leg and deem it okay enough to walk the rest of the way home. I might be limping, but I'm in one piece.

The walk back to the apartment is slow but steady. Each hobbled step brings me closer to the comfort of my home.

Gingerly, I take the stairs one step at a time, careful to ensure I don't take another tumble.

Sweaty and red-faced from my walk, I breathe a sigh of relief once I make it to the landing and my door comes into view. The image of me in a long, hot bubble bath beckons but the note taped to the front door has me pausing.

*You and me. Tonight. Be ready— Your sexy neighbor.*

I've made a terrible mistake in making any sort of contact with this man.

"Yeah. I don't think so, buddy," I mumble, tearing off the note and hobbling inside.

I gave Kane an inch and he's taking the whole damn mile. I asked for his help related to all things dating, but he's made it his mission to disrupt my life. First with his motorcycle and now with his *fucking magical* tongue.

*Nope. Don't go there.* I sigh. *Too late.*

Charlie watches me with blatant judgment in his eyes from his spot on the back of the couch as I slam the door and lean against it. Thoughts of the other night playing out like a movie behind my eyelids.

Yeah, definitely cannot go anywhere with him tonight. I don't think I could look him in the eye again without picturing him between my legs, grinning up at me like a devil before diving back in.

The shower wasn't as helpful as I thought it'd be. My injuries stung even more under the hot spray as I cleaned them. Once the pain subsided all I could think of while the water cascaded down my body was Kane's hands caressing every part of me. Then I imagined what he'd look like naked and in my shower.

Yeah, the shower didn't help at all.

Kane can try all he wants, but I'm not going anywhere with him. I need a quiet night at home far away from him and all the feelings that rise to the surface when he's around.

Freshly washed and bandaged, I grab my yarn and knitting needles and get back to my scarf-making. Charlie bats at one of his toys on the floor, the tiny little bell jingling as he does.

"You just had to start that right now, huh? I hope you're proud of yourself." As usual, Charlie gives zero shits about my complaining and continues batting away at the toy.

The needles make a satisfying click and scrape as I work away, my sole focus being every pull of the yarn through the hole.

Knitting has a calming effect on me and I feel the tension that was rising earlier drift away. At some point, Charlie abandons his toy and curls up against my legs, the ball of yarn resting by his pink nose.

The tell-tale sound of a motorcycle speeding through the neighborhood has my needles pausing as I turn my head to listen. When the engine grows louder, I can't help myself. I put aside my knitting and gracelessly push myself off the couch.

Charlie yawns, his little claws sticking out of his white feet as he stretches with all the empty space beside him.

Holding my breath, I gently lift apart the blinds and glance down to the parking lot below.

Kane removes his helmet tossing his dark wavy hair to the side. The engine's roar dies with the twist of a key before he pulls off his aviator sunglasses. Then, as if he knows I'm watching him, he looks directly at me white teeth gleaming as he smiles and winks.

How does he know I'm here? Surely he can't see me, right? Shit, does he know?

My heart pounds in my chest, a sinking feeling settling in my gut at being caught watching him. Wide-eyed, I whirl around to Charlie who sits on the couch watching me with his ginger head tilted at me.

"He didn't see me, right?" His green eyes squint at me, but because he's a fucking cat, he doesn't answer. "You're right," I say, crossing the room and taking him into my arms. "It doesn't matter, and you need all the cuddles right now." His ears tilt back as I kiss the top of his furry head trying to calm my racing heart.

Boots clomp up the stairs and I shut my eyes praying to whoever is listening that Kane doesn't stop at my door. Charlie purrs loudly against my chest, offering a bit of comfort in this stressful position I've put myself in.

Thankfully someone hears my plea and Kane keeps trudging past my door. I breathe a sigh of relief at the soft thud of his door closing next door.

"Whew, that was close, Charlie." He lets loose a loud meow before wiggling himself free from my hold.

Convinced Kane isn't coming back I sit back down, arranging the pillows around me like a fort of comfort, and continue my knitting. I'm about halfway done with the green scarf. If I focus, I could get this thing finished and start on something else. Maybe a hat or something. Come to think of it, a sweater would keep me occupied for a long, long time.

Just as I finish the final row, there's an unmistakable knock at my door. "I'm coming," I yell towards the door, my pillows falling to the floor as I maneuver out of them. I learned my lesson last time and I know that if I refuse to get up, he's just going to get louder.

Kane's laugh is muffled through the door. "That's funny, that's what you said the other night."

Angry, I whip the door open to see him standing in exactly the same pose the last time he was here, all leaning and sexy and dangerous.

"No, I didn't," I hiss, trying my hardest to keep from admiring his chest through his white t-shirt, the swirling tattoos peeking out from underneath the collar.

Kane doesn't even bother trying to hide his gaze as it sweeps down my body, pausing at my bandaged knee. "Else, what happened?"

His eyes have lost their playful gleam, concern taking its place. I ignore him, shuffling on my feet.

"I'm not going anywhere with you tonight," I say in case my pajama shorts and hoodie didn't make that clear enough.

Kane steps closer, filling my doorway. He places a large hand on my shoulder, pushing me to the side, and steps into my apartment.

"Tell me what happened." His face is set with a stern expression which is at odds with the playful one I'm familiar with.

Heat builds under my skin as I watch him confidently waltz into my apartment and remove his leather jacket before sinking onto my couch, both arms resting across the back. His lips quirk in a smug grin as if to say 'Yeah, I remember exactly what happened on this couch.'

Bastard.

"I fell." My arms cross under my boobs and I cock my hip. "Don't make barging into my apartment a habit. It's rude."

"Oh, Else," he sighs. "You can barge into my apartment anytime you want. I'm sure we'd both enjoy it."

"You're such an asshole."

He smiles at me, hazel eyes twinkling. "You love it."

"Debatable."

His gaze flicks down to my bandaged knee. "You using this as an excuse to not spend time with me? That hurts, Else."

I don't like his accusation, but he's not technically wrong.

"Despite what you think, this does hurt like hell." I point to my knee and show him my palms which resemble ground beef. "I think this gives me the right to stay home and tend to my wounds."

He leans forward pursing those delicious lips of his. My body betrays me and heat builds under my skin at his nearness. No matter how hard I try to push it away my body remembers our little tryst the other night.

Damn him.

"We were going to do a rerun of the other night at the bar..." his voice trails off as he contemplates a change of plans. "I guess we can reschedule." I sigh in relief. "But don't think you're going to get away with this again. I've got a lot of ideas brewing up here." He points to his head.

"Sure," I scoff.

He ignores my little jab humming to himself as he leans back into the cushions rubbing his jaw. "I guess we could scroll through your dating apps. It didn't work well last time, but you seem more comfortable with that."

"George was...fine." I feel like I have to defend myself. "Aside from his hobbies, the lackluster conversation, and that terrible kiss, it wasn't so bad."

He rolls his hazel eyes. "Right."

"Okay," I mumble, limping over to the couch, picking up wayward pillows as I go. "You were going to have me talk to guys again?"

Suddenly I'm glad my knee is torn up and bleeding. The thought of having to approach men again has my blood pressure rising.

That whole exchange at the bar was cringeworthy. Why he expected me to be fine with chatting with a table full of handsome men, I'll never know. I don't know what to say in those types of situations. Don't know how to act. Past experiences taught me to avoid them at all costs. Growing up in a larger body teaches you that lesson pretty quickly.

"You wanted my help, so that's what I'm doing." He never glances up from his phone, his thumb tapping away at the screen.

He's not wrong. I brought this all on myself. Desperation can be a real bitch sometimes.

"How's Chinese food sound?"

I shrug my shoulders. "Doesn't matter to me. Where are you ordering from?"

We argue over which take-out place has the better food, managing to narrow it down to two. Ultimately I won and I feel a tad smug about it.

Done ordering our food, he sets his phone on the side table and gestures to me closer. "Come here and pull up that dating app."

To try and keep my distance from him, I sat as far away from him as I could.

"Nah, I think I'm good here."

Kane rolls his eyes, his arm reaching across the cushions between us hooking under the crook of my knee and dragging me across the couch.

"Kane!" I screech holding onto the gold velvet pillow clutched over my stomach for dear life. He ignores me, tugging me closer until I'm practically in his lap, my injured leg thrown over his thigh.

"Can't see the screen from all the way over there," he explains, his eyes glued to my bandaged knee. His large hands settle on my leg, one on my upper thigh while the other casually strokes the skin along my shin.

*Don't think about the other night. Don't think about the other night.*

Kane's soft question pierces my thoughts. "Does it hurt?"

Does what hurt? His hands on my skin? "Huh?" I ask, momentarily stunned.

"You're knee. Does it hurt?" The hand on my thigh squeezes.

Great, the last thing I need is to become self-conscious of my thunder thighs. He gently grabs my hand flipping it over and tenderly running a finger across each scape.

Something feels like it's lodged in my throat at the tender way he touches me and I clear my throat before slowly pulling my hand free from his.

Needing to distract myself from how close he is and how hard my heart pounds, I pull out my phone and scroll through my apps searching for the dating app.

"It did. It feels better now than it did when I was walking home. At least it's stopped bleeding." My shoulders shrug. It actually hurts like a bitch and I can barely bend my knee, but I won't tell him that. For all the sharp pain the cuts on my palm caused, they've dulled down to a soft simmer.

The app has finally loaded and I hold my phone up between us. "Okay, here it is."

He reaches for my phone. "At least tell me the other guy looks worse."

"Yeah," I say sarcastically, "I showed the sidewalk who's boss."

He chuckles softly before getting straight to business.

If I thought I was picky, Kane is downright finicky. He only looks at a profile for two seconds before vetoing the poor man.

Lucky for me, he's not controlling my phone. I learned quickly that if I wanted a say in who he swipes on, I had to be the one in control of the phone.

"What's wrong with this one?" I ask for the millionth time tonight. Discarded food containers are sprawled across the ottoman as we sit on the couch eating and scrolling through profiles. "He's good-looking, has a nice job, he even listed bungee jumping as a bucket list item."

"Seriously?" he says through a mouthful of eggroll. "He's holding up a fish like a trophy. Pass." He swallows his food and takes a drink of water. "And what's with the bungee jumping thing?"

We've been going at this for what seems like hours, arguing back and forth over which way to swipe, only taking a break when the food showed up.

My fork twirls in the Lo Mein noodles in an attempt to shove as many of them in my mouth as possible. I guess I'm no better than Kane when it comes to talking with my mouth full.

"It's something I always wanted to do. I'm scared of heights though so it's more about getting the courage to actually do it. That's why it's a bucket list item. And," I add for argument's sake, "almost every guy has a picture with a fish."

"My point exactly."

I scoff and roll my eyes before tossing my phone to the side. "I've had enough swiping for one night. Hand me the remote." I reach across his chest making a gimme gesture.

Kane hasn't let me stray far from his side all night, only taking his hands off my leg to eat. He wouldn't even let me get my own food, practically shoving me back down on the couch and threatening to tie me down if I got up. The mental image I got from that made me blush.

The remote clicks as I find my preferred platform and start the next episode of my comfort show.

Kane settles deeper into the couch, his arm resting across my shoulder, my injured leg still tossed over his. "What's this?"

I sit up, shocked. "You've never seen this show? Have you been living under a rock?"

"For fucks sake, calm down. No, I haven't seen it. Is it new?" His hand squeezes my shoulder, lightly pulling me back down to the couch.

"No, it's not new. It's been around for a while. I'm pretty sure I was in college when it first started. A whole bunch of us would gather around the TV in the dorm commons and watch it while eating junk food."

"Sounds nice," his thumb gently brushes across my shoulder. "But that's why I've never seen it. When you join the military, you don't have much free time." He sucks in a deep breath, kicking his feet up on the ottoman. "What's it about?"

My gaze flickers over to him, his eyes glued to the screen. I didn't know he was in the military, but based on the way he said it, I don't think he wants to talk about it. So instead of trying to drag information out of him, I explain the premise of the show and decide to start it from the first episode. That way he can properly enjoy the tension between my favorite characters from the very beginning.

We sit together on the couch laughing at the hilarity of the show's dynamic. The later it gets, the more soothing Kane's laughter becomes and I have a hard time keeping my eyes open before they slip closed entirely.

# Chapter Eight

*Kane*

This morning I woke up cuddled against Elsie on her couch. We were completely wrapped around each other. Elsie's head rested on my chest, her leg tucked between mine, and my hand gripping her ass.

The evidence of how much I enjoyed our cuddle session was dangerously close to poking her in the stomach.

What the hell am I getting myself into?

First, I went down on her— and gladly would again—and now I wake up surrounded by her. I don't know what's worse, the fact that I spent a night with my neighbor or the fact that I enjoyed it.

And want to do it again.

A metallic clang rings through the garage cutting through the fog of my thoughts. I'm so occupied thinking about Elsie that I've stopped paying attention to my work.

Bill hollers at me for my clumsiness from the next bay, his coveralls smeared with grease, that toothless grin near infectious. I flip him a good-natured bird before getting back to work determined to stay focused.

It doesn't work. Within no time, my thoughts are back on my neighbor.

She's closed off, sure, but I'm slowly getting to see the person beyond the wall. She's more talkative than I thought she was. Elsie has this quiet charm about her that she hides most of the time.

Hell, I think I laughed more last night than I have in a while. I've never spent so much time with one woman in my entire life, and I'm finding that I like it. She may act like she hates me, but I know I'm growing on her just as much as she's growing on me.

Maybe too much.

A night out with Ash and Garrett should do the trick. Hell, Garrett's still probably on a boat in the middle of the ocean somewhere, but I know Ash will be up for anything.

Since I agreed to help with Elsie, he's been pestering me to be his wingman. Most nights we meet up with a group of friends or watch sports at the bar. I leave earlier than I used to and Ash has noticed. I think about Elsie sitting alone in her apartment and I can't do it. There's something about seeing that streak of light through her dark curtains that urges me home.

When I take my break from working on a beat-up Ford to text Ash, he doesn't hesitate. My shift ends in a few hours and we agree to meet up at the bar.

Curls pop loose from the bun I hastily threw it into before work this morning, tendrils slipping beneath my helmet and whipping me in the face as I drive through town to meet Ash.

The smell of smoke and beer fills my nostrils as I walk through our favorite place and order a drink. I can't stop thinking about Elsie as I wait for the pretty blonde bartender to pour my whisky and coke.

I wonder what Elsie thought when she woke up alone on the couch.

Does she know that we fell asleep in each other's arms?

What's she doing right now?

Maybe she's putting on one of her concerts. The thought pops a smile on my face.

The tumbler lands with a thud on the hardwood of the bartop. "You having a nice night?" She cocks her hip and leans in, her eyes dancing around my chest and up to my face. I haven't seen her working here before so she must be new.

Ice clinks against the glass as I bring it to my lips, not bothering to hide my smirk at her hungry eyes. "I'm sure it could be better," I say before the cool liquid slides down my throat.

She holds out a small hand and I take it. "Alex." Her hand is cold from the drinks she serves and I introduce myself to her. "Kane," she repeats my name with a seductive smile. "You know," she drawls leaning forward, "that name fits." Her sultry eyes travel up and down the expanse of my chest before lingering on my lips.

She's giving me all the signs that she's interested, but for some reason, Elsie's face comes to mind.

I wonder what she'd look like giving me that smile.

A slap on the shoulder saves me from having to come up with a response.

Ash settles on a barstool next to me. "Shit, man I'm surprised you didn't bail on me again." He waves down Alex and quickly places his order.

"Figured you needed a wingman with that ugly mug of yours."

Ash lowers his head, shaking it as he laughs. "Fuck you, dude."

I laugh at the lighthearted insult before slapping his shoulder and pointing to a table in the middle of the bar.

The man doesn't need any help when it comes to women. He's a good-looking guy with an edge that women seem to love.

I've known Ash and his brother Garrett for most of my life and they couldn't be more different. One brother went into the Navy and now works on super yachts while the other owns his own extreme sports business. One brother follows the rules while the other one bends them.

I toss my leather jacket against the back of the wooden chair before taking a seat. It's fairly early in the night, so the bar isn't as busy as it usually is. Maybe Elsie would come since it's not too crowded. It's the perfect time for her to get out and practice talking to people.

Unable to stop myself, I pull up her contact information that she begrudgingly gave me last night so I wouldn't have to leave notes taped to her door.

*Kane: Come to The Brick*

*Elsie: Why?*

*Kane: Cuz I want you here*

*Elsie: Again, why?*

*Kane: Just put on a dress and get over here*

She better know that if she doesn't show up here that I'm going to give her so much shit about it.

Or maybe I'll throw her over my shoulder and bring her here kicking and screaming myself.

The thought has a ring to it.

Ash sets down his glass with a thud before his chair scrapes against the floor. "What's got you smiling like that? Someone slip you a number already?" His head swivels as he looks around for the potential culprit.

"No." I pocket my phone before he can catch me. If he finds out I invited Elsie, he's liable to beat my ass. Sure, he'll know when she shows up—and she *will* show up— but it'll be too late for him to do anything about it unless he wants to look like a giant asshole.

"Damn, it is pretty slow tonight."

Which makes for the perfect opportunity for Elsie. It's nothing like the last time we were here, so I'm hoping she won't be as timid.

Ash and I enjoy our drinks as we catch up on everything that's been going on in recent weeks. His business keeps him pretty busy and if he's not working, he's playing. Off doing the next hair-brained, death-defying idea. Sometimes I think the man has a death wish.

We're on our second round of drinks when Ash slams his glass down and glares at me from across the table.

"You've got to be kidding me." I turn around looking to see what's got him all riled up.

Elsie's here and damn if she doesn't look like a ray of sun on a rainy day. She hasn't spotted me yet and I take the time to drink her in. I wasn't lying when I said she's a beautiful woman—she's stunning. The bangs she normally has pinned back frame her lovely face making her brown eyes seem bigger. Her sunshine yellow top has a plunging neckline, showing off the velvet smoothness of her chest. She didn't wear a dress, but I'm not complaining about the tight, ass-hugging black jeans she's wearing. And to think, I know exactly what that ass feels like in the palm of my hand.

For several moments, I'm stunned just looking at her. Breathless, almost.

"Over here, beautiful."

Elsie turns at the sound of my voice and a smile breaks across her face. There's a growing confidence in each step as she walks over to us. She's no longer rounding her shoulders or folding in on herself. She's radiant, shoulders back and head held high. Her eyes keep darting to the floor, but I'll give her time.

She sits in the chair I pulled out for her before rounding on me. "Next time, don't be so demanding," she chastises. "Hey, Ash."

Ash holds up his drink in greeting before taking a large gulp. "Nice to see you again, Elsie."

I know he's lying but at least he's playing nice.

"I wouldn't have to be so demanding if I could get you out of your house easier. You wouldn't have come otherwise. But I'm glad to see you're learning. If you didn't show up, I would've dragged you in"

The eye roll she throws my way has me chuckling. "As if you would ask nicely." She even earns a grin from Ash. "I need a drink," she sighs.

"What do you want?" I ask, my chair scraping against the floor as I stand. She gives a non-answer, saying to *surprise* her. I know the woman doesn't get out much, but surely she knows what kind of drink she likes.

There's a small group gathered around the bar and I gently wedge myself between people to wait to place my order. I watch as Alex flits around the bar taking orders and pouring drinks while thinking about what to order for Elsie.

Someone nudges my side, drawing my gaze.

"Oops, sorry about that." The girl barely comes to my shoulder as she swipes her short blonde hair out of her face. "Something must've popped out of the floor," she laughs, turning to look at the floor behind us.

"Yeah, you've gotta watch out for that concrete," I tease. She's cute, although a little young—she looks barely old enough to drink.

"Normally I'm very sure-footed." She leans on the bar next to me, a bar she's barely tall enough to lean on. "Have you been waiting long?"

My elbows hit the bar beside her as we wait. "A bit, but it looks like reinforcements are coming." Another bartender ties an apron around his waist and immediately gets to work and it doesn't take him long to reach us. He stops in front of me with a polite smile. "What can I get ya?"

Seeing as I have no idea what to order for Elsie, I point to the small blonde next to me. "She can go first."

"Oh, wow. Thanks." She orders some fruity-sounding drinks, so after he places them in front of her, I order the same thing for Elsie.

Girls love fruity drinks, right?

Ash is nursing what's left of his beer as I approach the table with drinks for all of us. Elsie, however, is nowhere to be seen.

"Where is she?" I ask hoping he didn't say something to upset her.

He shrugs his shoulders and downs the rest of his drinks. "Talking to some guy. I don't know what's going on with you two, but as soon as she saw you talking to that chick, she stood up and just walked over there."

I follow his line of sight and sure enough, Elsie stands next to a guy, her hand resting on his forearm. He looks like all the guys I shot down on that dating app last night. I'm sure this dude has a picture holding up a fish on his dating profile.

This is what I wanted right? Our deal was for me to help her date, so why is my chest filling with jealousy?

Her long hair slides behind her shoulder as she tilts her head back and laughs. The guy she's talking to watches her in a way I don't like.

He's looking at her like she's his next meal.

"Stop holding the beer hostage." In my jealous state, the drinks are still nestled in my hands, condensation beginning to loosen my grip.

My mood sours the longer the night drags on. Elsie eventually comes back to the table to grab her drink before walking across the bar to the man whose face I'd like to punch in. With the crowd starting to pick up, Ash eventually leaves me to go chat up the small blonde who was ordering drinks earlier leaving me alone to brood.

My eyes never stray from Elsie. Even when my drink empties, I don't bother ordering another one. I should be proud of the progress I'm seeing in her, but it's completely overshadowed by this unfamiliar feeling.

A feeling that lingers long after I follow her home.

# Chapter Nine

*Elsie*

"Hold on tight," Kane instructs before zooming out of the parking lot. I've learned to have a death grip around his waist whenever I ride with him. My first ride on his motorcycle was a lesson I don't think I'll ever forget.

It's been two weeks since the incident at the bar and things between Kane and I have been tense.

It's my own fault though. I guess I read into his invite to the bar the other night, and when he was smiling at that gorgeous, petite blonde woman, I let my feelings get in the way. When I saw Paul looking over at me, my reluctance snapped. I walked over to him without a word to Ash— not that he seemed to mind.

Paul's nice and he seems interested in me. He's no Kane, but he's attractive in a normal, average way. He's pretty straight-laced—a button-up and slacks type of guy with an office job where the most adventurous thing he does is a pub crawl with his old college friends once a month. We exchanged numbers, but nothing more happened.

Especially not when Kane was watching every move I made with a scowl on his face.

He stopped by the apartment last night looking rumpled and sexy to tell me that he was taking me somewhere today. All he said was, "Wear tennis shoes and pull your hair up." So I did. I have no clue where we're going or what we're doing, but I know that I trust him.

We've spent most of our nights together in my living room watching shows or talking. If someone had told me a month ago that the highlight of my day would be when my neighbor came over to hang out, I wouldn't believe it. Yet it's the truth.

While he's infuriating at times, he's a lot of fun to be around. You know, aside from the overwhelming attraction to him I can't seem to get under control.

The mid-afternoon sun warms the leather jacket Kane made me wear when he saw my tank top. He wrapped it around me and muttered about safety before letting me get on the bike.

I won't complain that now his sculpted arms and tanned skin are fully on display. And damn it, I can't get the memory of those arms wrapped around me while we slept peacefully on the couch, all warm and safe.

My feelings towards him, which were once annoyance, have shifted into an area I'm not comfortable digging too deeply into. He didn't sign up for me to start crushing on him. I try to play it off, but I think he can see right through the snarky remarks only made to keep my growing feelings hidden.

I'm not sure how long I can convince myself that we're just friends. That I don't think about him when my hand slips into my shorts every night as I lay in bed. That there isn't something blooming in my chest at the thought of him.

My head rests on his strong back as he drives us farther away from town until we pull into a parking lot in front of a building. I don't catch the sign as Kane passes it, but the words adventure sports stick out.

Where the hell has he brought me?

Kane's hands settle on my hips as he helps me off his motorcycle. His hazel eyes sparkle at me, his mouth upturned in a self-satisfied grin.

"Where are we?" I ask, trying desperately not to think about how close we're standing or the fact that I want to climb him like a tree right now with the way he's looking at me.

"Two words for you, Else. Bucket. List."

He reaches under my chin and unsnaps the helmet placing it on the seat before sliding his jacket off my shoulders. It may be my overactive imagination, but I swear he let his palms linger on my skin a moment too long.

"You mean—" He reaches for my hand and clasps it tightly in his as he drags me to the entrance.

"Yep."

Immediately my heart begins to race, pounding in my chest like a stampede of elephants. I can't believe he's brought me here.

I can't believe he *listened* to me for once.

Everyone has a bucket list, right? But I didn't, for one second, ever think about crossing something off it. How could I, when everything on there is so far outside of my comfort zone? Bungee jumping, flying an airplane, eating a croissant in Paris... Everything so far outside the four comfortable walls of my apartment.

Kane holds open the door as the cool air blasts into me. My eyes widen when I take in who's standing behind the counter.

Ash smoothly strides around the counter to greet us, a quiet hi for me and a back-slapping hug for Kane.

"You guys ready for this?" He asks with an excited grin, rubbing his palms together.

I'm sure I look like a fish with my mouth open as I take everything in. There's stuff everywhere. My eyes pinball around the building noticing equipment for sale, safety gear, and a multitude of clothing hanging on racks. Kayaks and canoes hang above us on the ceiling and helmets of every kind are displayed on a wall next to life vests, ropes, and goggles. There's something new everywhere I look.

"Hell yeah," Kane agrees, pulling me closer and resting a hand on my hip.

Ash looks at me and my bewildered expression and chuckles. "Great." He hands us both a clipboard with all sorts of legal jargon for us to sign as he explains everything. "I've got everything in the truck and the guys are already out there setting it all up." We follow him through the side door and out to a dusty white truck. "It's about a five-minute drive out to the ravine. It'll be a bit bumpy so be prepared."

Ravine?

Bumpy?

My throat works to swallow, my nerves setting me on edge. Silently, I climb into the back seat, eying the four-point harness instead of a seat belt. Kane must see the expression on my face because he closes the front passenger door and opens mine before leaning in and adjusting the buckles. I try to not think about how much adjusting he has to do and stare at the ceiling instead.

"You doin' okay, Else?" he asks, his voice soft and concerned. His knuckles rub against the skin of my chest as he fits the straps and I focus on his touch and not what's waiting for me at the ravine. "You look like you're contemplating an escape plan. It's either that or my murder," he snorts.

The smack that lands on his chest doesn't faze him one bit. "Not murder," I manage to grit out. Breathing deeply through my nose, I slowly let it out. "I'm trying to not die of a heart attack right now thank you very much."

His eyebrows knit together. "I thought you wanted to do this?"

"I do—" I start before swallowing. "It's a surprise is all."

He snaps the buckle and smiles at me. "That's kind of the point here, Else. I figured you'd lock me out of your apartment if I told you and you'd refuse to come," he adds.

He's one hundred percent correct but I'm not going to tell him that.

Kane gives my thigh a reassuring squeeze before he closes my door and buckles himself in the seat next to Ash.

It doesn't take long for me to understand exactly why there are harnesses instead of seatbelts in the truck. Ash was being generous when he called the ride "bumpy." It's more like driving over boulders with how much I'm jostled from side to side and I find myself thankful that Kane kept the harness tight across my chest so I'm not being thrown around like a rag doll.

The two men in the front whoop and holler the entire ride. From the sound of their laughter, you'd think we were on a rollercoaster and not being threatened to roll the vehicle at every turn.

The second the truck rolls to a stop in front of the ravine, I toss the straps loose and throw myself onto solid ground.

Not that I'll be on it much longer...

Ash introduces us to Joel and Abe who set out the equipment and go through the safety protocols. In what seems like no time, Kane and I are harnessed up with helmets strapped under our chins.

Kane's all smiles while anticipation swirls heavily in my gut. I've always wanted to do something like this.

*Not something*, I remind myself.

*This.*

I've been wanting to do *this* my whole life.

Joel and Abe guide us to the platform we'll be jumping from and I make the mistake of looking down.

Down.

Down.

And fucking down.

It's probably hundreds of feet deep with water glistening at the bottom in the mid-afternoon sun.

"Is now a bad time to tell you I'm afraid of heights?" I swallow down the growing fear and focus on Kane's hazel eyes.

"Don't back out on me now, Else." His hands stroke over my arms reassuringly while the guys triple-check the carabiners, tugging on our restraints, and hooking us up to the cord. The breath that I suck in is ragged to my ears and Kane pulls me to his chest. "Just keep breathing," he whispers in my ear as he holds me, "I've got you."

Everything goes distant. Even the men's voices are muffled as they give more directions but it's like trying to listen while underwater. Everything except Kane's voice rumbling in my ear. His strong arms pull me even tighter against him, our bodies flush as he instructs for the second time today to hold on tight.

My whole body is shaking and I can't seem to steady myself. Excitement verging on panic sweeps over me and I tilt my head up, looking into the eyes of the man whom I never saw coming, never dreamed of having.

Kane smiles softly down at me, kissing my forehead before we tumble over the edge.

# Chapter Ten

*Kane*

If I died in this moment, I'd die a happy man.

Elsie's bravery—although I know she's shitting herself inside—has pride swelling in my chest at how far she's come. She's fucking terrified, but I know this is something she wants, otherwise, she would've kicked and screamed like a wildcat when the guys started putting the harnesses on.

Emotions swam in those brown eyes as she looked up at me, so trusting that I couldn't help myself. The kiss on her forehead was unplanned, like most of my life when it comes to her, but I needed to give her one last part of myself before I threw us over the edge.

My stomach drops, that familiar sensation sending tingles down my spine, the wind rushing past us as we plunge into the ravine below. My joy can't be contained and thrilled shouts leave my throat almost drowning out Elsie's high-pitched screams.

I feel the moment we hit the end of the cord as it fights against gravity, stretching to its limit before flinging us back up. Elsie's shouts have turned into joyous laughter, her arms wrapped around me like a vise. We bounce several more times, our bodies flipping gracelessly into the air until we swing slightly, our momentum from the jump finally giving out.

Blood rushes to our faces, but that doesn't seem to bother Elsie. A grin spreads from ear to ear as she shakes with contagious laughter. "That was so fucking fun!" she squeals, all the fear before the jump now gone.

She's glowing, happiness radiating off her like sunshine, and I can't help myself. Elsie's looking at me in that way that has my breath stopping and I can't take it anymore. I cup her head in my hands and bring my mouth to hers.

We haven't kissed in weeks, and it's like giving water to a dying man. She's everything I need. The *only* thing I need at this moment. We're hanging upside down hundreds of feet in the air, but she's the only thing stealing my breath.

Her lips are soft and delectable against mine. I haven't realized how much I've been starved for this woman, longed for this woman until now. A soft whimper escapes her as our tongues tease together and it urges me on even more.

She tastes like fucking nirvana.

The rope jolts, breaking our lips apart as Abe and Joel haul us back to the platform. Elsie laughs, a sound I'm quickly becoming addicted to.

The several minutes it took for them to hoist us back onto the platform wasn't long enough. I don't want Elsie to leave my arms. I've enjoyed having her soft curves pressed tight against me, almost too much. Having her this close is highly distracting and addictive.

The guys help us find our balance, pulling us away from the edge before they start unhooking all the harnesses and cables.

"How was it?" Abe asks with a big grin. He's one of those extreme athletes that Ash hired in exchange for sponsorship. All he has to do is work a couple of days a week and he's bankrolled.

Elsie bounces on the balls of her feet, her eyes wide. "That was amazing," she enthuses. "I can see why people get addicted to it," she admits with a chuckle.

Joel unclips a carabiner. "Sounds like we got another thrill junkie on our hands."

Elsie dives into a conversation about other death-defying things she could do as Ash catches my eye. He's been like a shadow as Joel and Abe did their jobs getting us all hooked up, but now he's watching me with a curious eye.

When recognition crosses his features, I lift a brow in question.

The blonde in Ash's brown hair glimmers in the sun as he shakes his head, dismissing me. Something about his expression makes me want to ask more, but Elsie's laugh pulls my attention back to her.

Elsie's on cloud nine right now. She chats animatedly with Abe and I find myself staring at her, loving how her eyes sparkle.

I'm glad I could do this for her. When she said she wanted to go bungee jumping as part of her bucket list, I was a bit surprised. The woman who barely leaves her apartment wants to throw herself over a cliff? But seeing her now, I made the right call by setting this all up. Ash was a little reluctant when I said who it was for, but ultimately he caved.

Today has been revealing. Elsie's reservations from earlier have melted away and I'm seeing her bloom in front of my eyes. As she chats with the guys, I enjoy the view of her with the backdrop of the ravine.

It's strange to think she was only my quiet neighbor and now she's transformed into something else.

Her hair sticks out of its ponytail, little wisps of her bangs coming free as she shifts her attention to me. Those brown eyes are bright with excitement. She arches an eyebrow at me in question.

"What?" I ask with a chuckle. "You look like you're up to no good."

"Maybe I am." She turns to look at the ravine behind her. "I think I want to go again. Is that crazy?"

Joel calls out from the platform where he carefully resets the rope. "Go for it!"

"Yeah?" she calls back cupping her hands over her eyes to block the sun. "You'd let me do it?"

"Fuck yeah. I'm all for welcoming new junkies."

Elsie turns back to me, face questioning. I cross my arms over my chest and smirk when her eyes linger there. "This is all about you, Else. If you want to jump, jump. The only thing stopping you is you."

She bounces on her heel biting her lip as she thinks. I watch transfixed on her face as the corners of her mouth stretch in a smile. "Okay. I'm going to jump again."

I don't think I've ever been more proud of anyone than I am right now.

We both jumped solo before we needed to pack up. Else screeched and squawked the whole way down which was far more hysterical from up here. Ash and I were clutching our stomachs with laughter gaining chastising looks from Else when we started to tease her.

The ride back is a completely different story. Gone is the shaking mess she was at the start of the day, replaced by utter happiness. Hearing her laughter in the backseat as we bounce back to the main building has me grinning like a fool.

We say a quick goodbye to Ash and get back on the bike to head into town. Elsie sighs, her head resting on my shoulder, and wraps her arms tenderly around my waist. The urge to hold her tighter and kiss her forehead is foreign. One that won't seem to fade.

The afternoon quickly faded into the evening while we were having fun, the sun starting to set on our drive home. The two-lane highway between Ash's business and home is a quiet stretch of road, the warm air making for a great ride.

We turn around a curve in the road and instinctually the bike begins to slow. On the side of the road pulled over on the shoulder are two teenagers peering into the hood of a car.

Elsie sits up to peer around my shoulder as we come to a stop. "What's going on?"

I cut the engine and get off the bike. "I'm going to go see what I can do. You good to stay here?"

Her eyes snag on the teenage girl sitting in the grass before she reaches for my hand and throws her leg over the motorcycle. "I'll go sit with her." Her hand rests on my upper arm, her brown eyes soft as she looks at me. "Take your time. I'm in no rush." Elsie walks over to the girl, making polite introductions while I round the hood of the car.

The poor kid breathes a sigh of relief when I tell him I'm a mechanic. We chat while I fiddle with the engine, running through basic checks before thinking of bigger problems. He asks questions while I work, wanting to know what I'm looking for so he knows what to do next time. It doesn't take long to see the problem. Luckily it's an easy fix and within several minutes the engine purrs without a problem.

"Oh shit. Thanks, man," the teenager, Chase, calls from around the driver's side door. I wave politely as the hood slams shut before looking for Else.

She and the girl are sitting in the grass engrossed in polite conversation. It seems like Elsie's listening rather than talking, nodding in agreement at what the girl says. She must sense my gaze because she glances my way and smiles as her cheeks blush.

Never did I imagine the hermit next door smiling at me would send a rush through me. I wink back at her, loving the pink coloring her cheeks once more.

The teenage girl bounces up on her feet and claps, her voice high-pitched and bubbly as she yells her thanks, jogging past me to the car. Elsie watches me, her eyes sliding down my body as I stand in front of her and offer my greasy hands. She doesn't hesitate, clasping her hands in mine as I pull her to her feet.

"You know," she says, her hips swiveling as she wipes the grass off her ass, "you're a really good guy."

"How nice of you to notice," I scoff, handing her her helmet.

"You're nice," she amends, "but I mean you're a good man. I don't know many people who would've stopped to help."

My shoulders shrug as I adjust myself on my bike. "I help when and where I can. Doesn't make me a hero or anything."

She settles behind me, her hands resting on my shoulders. "Well, you're a hero to me," she whispers into my ear before kissing my cheek.

• • • •

AFTER OUR IMPROMPTU stop, we decided to get dinner. There was a small diner that Elsie deemed adorable and insisted we stop. We might've spent the entire day together, but not for one second did I wish to be somewhere else. With someone else.

I might've driven a bit slower on the way home just to keep her arms banded around me one minute longer.

It's completely dark by the time we get to the apartment and I find myself not wanting to leave her. My time with Elsie has been my highlight these past weeks and I want to spend as much time with her as I can.

She's all I think about. If I'm not thinking about her, I'm thinking about what I can do with her. My nights once filled with cheap flirting and hollow hookups are a thing of the past, and not one part of me misses it. There's something to be said about coming home to the same person. Someone who has started to feel like home to me.

My chest tightens the closer we get to her doorway, my thoughts solely focused on the feelings suddenly swirling in my heart, the realization that I'm building something special with her making my heart quicken.

She stops in front of her door, quickly unlocking it before she turns to face me. It's become a habit for us, like our nightly routine, for me to wait until she's safely inside before I leave. Most of the time she's dying to send me home, but I know it's all in jest. She enjoys having me near as much as I enjoy being with her.

"Kane," she pauses, her hands knitting together in front of her. "I can't tell you how much today meant to me."

Those brown eyes lock with mine, and I swear my heart stops. I have no right to feel the way I do. She's not mine and I'm not hers. But God, do I want her to be.

"Else, I hope you know I'd do anything for you," I admit, stepping closer to her. Her chest heaves, almost brushing against my own as she swallows hard.

"Would you like to come inside?"

I've been to her apartment many times, but not once has she asked me to come in. Most of the time, I barge right in knowing she'd complain about it, loving it when she gets flustered. But this question is riddled with meaning. Because we both know it's more than her asking me inside.

My hands rest on either side of her head, lightly caging her in. "You and I both know we won't be watching any shows tonight. If I walk in through this door, I won't be able to keep my hands off you. Fuck, it's hard enough already," I admit with clenched fists.

Her gaze never wavers. She blinks slowly once, twice, before setting her shoulders. "Kane, would you like to come inside?"

# Chapter Eleven

*Elsie*

I can't believe I said that. Scratch that, I can believe I said it, I'm just shocked that I did.

Kane reacts like a spring being let loose. One minute we're inches apart with tension coiled under our skin, the next his mouth is diving for mine. This kiss is all passion. The dam that has held back our attraction finally gives way in a torrent of emotion. He kisses me with such ferocity and tenderness that for a moment, I don't know how to react.

I've known that I want him—have wanted him— for a long time. Every time he steps into my space, teases, or touches me is a reminder of how much I want him. Maybe I've been watching him all these years, loathing him because I wanted him and knew he would never want me.

Never be mine.

But fuck is he proving me wrong, if only for a moment. Because right now? Right now it's almost tangible. Believable.

His strong hands caress my every curve until they squeeze my ass. Goosebumps pop up on my skin as his mouth breaks away from mine, his lips skimming along the sensitive skin of my neck. I'm so lost in the feeling of him, that I don't notice the whimper leave my lips. Or that my hands are now tugging on the soft curls of his hair, pulling it loose from its tie.

Kane's breath tickles my ear. "Let's get you inside." His playful nip at my earlobe has me smacking his chest. The grin he gives me has my heart threatening to stop beating. He's sexy and disheveled and the way he's looking at me right now is how I've always wanted a man to look at me.

Like I'm the most precious thing he's ever seen.

He grabs my hand as he opens my door, pulling me into the quiet darkness of the apartment. Out of habit, I look for Charlie, but he's nowhere to be seen. He must've heard Kane's voice and taken off running. Not that I blame him.

I'm in uncharted territory. I haven't brought a man into this apartment in like...*ever*. Kane doesn't count, hasn't counted, until now and I don't know where to go from here, what to do. All the romance novels I've read don't explain how the couple goes from point A to point B—or maybe they did and I was so lost in the moment that I didn't notice.

Fuck, why wasn't I paying more attention?

Kane saves me from my inner turmoil, bringing our clasped hands to his mouth and kissing my hand softly.

"Care to show me your room, Else? The couch was fun last time, but I want to see you sprawled before me like a damn feast."

Now that he's brought up the couch, a heavy and demanding pulsing starts in my core and I clench my thighs together as if that would help.

There's never been a man in my room and now that Kane's in it, it feels small. The lamp on the bedside table clicks on, the soft light illuminating the large man in front of me. In typical Kane fashion, he walks around my room, examining my small knick-knacks.

My room is my little cave. The walls are a deep emerald green, my queen-sized bed taking up most of the space. Pillows of all shapes and sizes cover the bed, the duvet barely visible beneath them.

Kane shakes his head. "So many fucking pillows."

"What's wrong with my pillows?" I ask, defensive of my space while plopping on the bed. He rounds the bed stopping in front of me, his hands resting on either side of my hips as he leans over me.

"Nothing," he whispers, sending shivers down my spine. "I've just got to put them to good use."

The question about what, exactly, he means by that dies in my throat as he kisses me. It's only been a matter of minutes since the last time his mouth was on mine, but it feels like a whirlwind every time.

Kane kisses his way down my neck sliding the straps of my top down my shoulders, leaving more skin for him to explore.

Everything he's doing is so different from what I've experienced before. He's taking his time with me. Focusing solely on me. Not that many men, or man, took their time to learn what I wanted, what I liked. How to touch me.

But he did.

He does.

Kane's tongue caresses the top of my breasts and my hands slide into his hair, holding him close to me. I want him to devour me, consume me whole as waves of desires crash over me.

"Off," he growls. "I want this off." He leans back, trying to tug my top free from where it's tucked into my jeans. When it doesn't come loose, his face scrunches up in confusion.

"It's a bodysuit," I chuckle. "I have to take my pants off first."

"By all means then," he grins, replacing my spot on the bed when I stand. "Don't let me stop you." He's all arrogant as he leans back on his elbows, his gaze flicking up and down my body as I undress in front of him.

He's seen me naked before, hell he's put his mouth on my body where no one else has bothered to, but self-consciousness is a greedy bitch.

My hands pause on the button of my jeans, my eyes looking down at the roundness of my belly. I've seen some of the girls he brings home and I'm nothing like them. No flat stomach or legs for days.

I'm just me.

The bed creaks and Kane stands before me, his fingers tilting my chin until my eyes meet his. He runs his hand through my hair, brushing my bangs away from my face. "Else, what happened? Where'd you go?"

My head is screaming at me to keep my mouth closed, to not ask the question hanging on the edge of my tongue, but I have to know.

"Kane," I breathe, hoping that I'm not about to ruin everything. "Are you sure you want me? I—"

"Stop it." His voice is sharp, cutting through my growing embarrassment. "Don't you say another fucking word, Elsie. For fucks sake. Of course, I want you. You're all I can fucking think about. No, don't you dare look away." His hands cup my face as he steps closer, blocking everything but him. "You deserve to be told how much you're wanted. God, Elsie, you're amazing and should be told every day. If you think I don't want to worship every curve of your goddamn body. If you think I don't want to run my tongue down every inch of your skin, then how can I show you how much I want you? You're all I can see. Only you." Gently, he kisses my lips, my cheeks, my neck. "Let me show you how much I want you. You, Elsie. No one else."

Warmth blooms in my chest, a feeling I've been denying myself for so long. There's no use fighting what I've started to feel for him.

But it's a daydream.

A wish.

Here for a moment, gone the next.

This might be the only time I feel cherished, so I'll be damned if I get in my own way. Determined to live in the moment and not dwell on what comes next, I nod in agreement fighting back the brimming tears determined to hide them.

Kane wastes no time ridding me of my jeans, scowling when he gets to my bodysuit. I giggle at his flustered expression.

"What?" I ask. "A piece of clothing the great Kane can't take off? I'm shocked."

A sharp sting radiates from my ass cheek where Kane's hand landed. "I'm a quick learner. Now get it off."

He watches as it slides over my skin, his eyes watching every movement. Once it hits the floor, Kane is on me, his hands sliding over my curves removing my underwear as he goes until I'm standing naked in front of him.

Swallowing thickly, I tug his shirt over his head, exploring the muscled expanse of his chest. He's so beautiful it's almost painful to look at. Tattoos paint his chest, shoulders, and arms in a patchwork of breathtaking art. He shudders when I gently kiss the center of his chest loving the feeling of his arms tightening around me.

Every touch is carefully stored, protected, and safeguarded in my memory. For once in my life, I'm going to live in the moment.

Kane doesn't seem to mind that I'm taking my time. His hands trace circles on my skin, touching me where he can while I explore his body until he's standing naked before me.

His beauty knocks the breath from my lungs.

How in the world can this man want me?

"Else," his voice is deep and rough, cutting through the tension building in my bedroom as he hooks his hands around my thighs and throws me on the bed, his body covering mine like a blanket. The stubble of his beard contrasts with the silky smooth kisses against my skin as he nips and sucks his way down my body. He stops at the small swells of my breasts sucking my nipples into his mouth, his tongue swiping over the sensitive peaks. My chest heaves with every heavy breath.

His hair tickles my round stomach as he works his way lower. He touches me like I'm a precious gift, so tender that it has tears welling in my eyes.

Live in the moment.

Don't think about tomorrow or what it will bring.

The reminder that this won't be something I'll experience again draws me back to the here and now.

My legs are thrown over his shoulders, my only warning before he spreads my folds and licks. The wet warmth of his tongue sucks the breath from my lungs, his movements lazy and unrushed. Kane hums in satisfaction, the vibrations adding a whole new sensation, my body relaxing into his touch.

"Damn, Else," he praises. "You taste so fucking good." I swear my eyes roll into the back of my head, a drawn-out moan my only response to his words. He chuckles against my sensitive flesh sending fresh waves of pleasure pooling in my belly.

Every swipe of his tongue, the alternating pressure when he swirls his tongue over my clit has my back arching off the bed.

He's the master over my body, commanding it to do his bidding.

His fingers sink into my core, my muscles clenching around him in reflex. Unhurried, Kane stokes that flame of desire, taking me right to the edge without pushing me over. I'm on the edge of that cliff once again, our bodies pressed tight together in another kind of fall. Only this time I'm not jumping off the cliff, I'm falling into his arms.

My head lifts off the mattress when his lips kiss the soft skin of my inner thigh before Kane settles on his knees between my spread legs and pushes himself off the bed. "Where are you going?"

"Don't worry, Else," he says over his shoulder with a crooked grin. "I'm not going anywhere."

He rummages through the pocket of his jeans until he pulls out his wallet, the wrapper of the condom shining in the soft lamplight.

The bed dips from his weight as he kneels between my thighs. His eyes devour me as he brings the wrapper to his mouth and rips it open with his teeth.

Fuck. That's the sexiest thing I've ever seen.

In a matter of moments, Kane settles himself between my hips, his lips finding mine in a desperate kiss. My body is riddled with anticipation, waiting on bated breath from him to finally sink into me. Instead, he sits up reaching behind my head.

"So many fucking pillows," he repeats the phrase from earlier shaking his head. "Lift your hips." I do as he says, still a bit confused as to what he's doing until I feel the soft suede of one of my decorative pillows sliding underneath me.

So that's what he means.

Satisfied with his work, he grins down at me, my body at an odd angle with my hips higher than my chest. I don't feel pretty in this position, but the look he's giving me could set the world on fire. "Perfect." He lifts my leg and nibbles on my knee before notching himself at my entrance.

My world stops. My mind spinning as fantasy meets reality.

Kane's hazel eyes lock with mine as he slides home. We both gasp as he pushes himself to the hilt, my body adjusting to his size. Nothing, no one, has felt as good as Kane does. The angle of my hips has him hitting a sensitive spot inside me, a shiver of pleasure tingling down my spine at the contact.

His fingers dig into my soft hips, his gaze focusing on where our bodies are connected as he begins to move. I watch as the strong muscles of his abdomen flex with every thrust, the sight one I thought I'd never see.

Every rock of his hips into mine has me seeing stars. How have I gone so long without this? My eyes slide closed, a whirlwind of sensation threatening to drown me.

"No, Else," he grits out through clenched teeth. "Keep those eyes on me. Watch what I'm doing to you. Watch what you do to me." He swivels his hips, reaching that special place as I whimper, my eyes snapping up to his.

Now I know why those women scream his name, because damn it, his name is falling from my lips in prayer. "Kane. You feel so good," I manage to say through gasps of pleasure. He doubles his efforts, pounding faster and deeper with each thrust. My ankles lock around his waist loving the feel of his tight ass flexing as he moves.

"That's it, Else. Fuck, you look so beautiful taking my cock."

"Yes," I groan, my head digging into the mattress.

His hand snakes down between my legs expertly finding my clit and swiping his thumb over the sensitive nub. The sounds that escape my lips are otherworldly. But I'm not the only one hanging on by a thread. Kane's praises and grunts mingle with mine as sweat covers our bodies.

With a sudden cry, my orgasm barrels through me, knocking the breath from my lungs, my muscles clenching around his length as he buries himself deep inside me. I'm completely undone by him.

Kane's deep moan settles around me as he spills himself in me. His head falls to my soft belly, both of us panting heavily as our bodies settle.

How I'm going to move past this moment, this feeling, I don't know.

But I have to.

# Chapter Twelve

*Elsie*

K ane isn't here.

The room smells faintly of him, but the other half of the bed is empty, the sheets cold.

I guess I had no expectations about what would happen *after* we had sex, but it still stings. We had no agreement beyond him helping me with my dating life, so it's not like I have any claim to him.

But things were said...

I can hear his voice in my head, the echo of words seared into my memory. They'll always be tucked in the back of my mind to serve as a reminder that at one moment in time, someone said they wanted me.

I can't hold him to whispered words shared in a moment of passion.

If there's one thing I know from reading my books, people say things they don't mean. Especially in bed.

With a groan, I roll over burying my face in the pillows. I knew this would happen, didn't I? I told myself not to think about tomorrow, and tomorrow's here.

I don't regret anything. Not a single second. But my feelings for Kane are going to be a problem. He's not a relationship guy, and I'm a relationship kind of girl. He's the guy that goes out to pick up girls and helps people when they need it. I'm another project to him.

Although everything I know about Kane screams otherwise, it's the one thing I have to protect myself. He can't want me. He doesn't want me. He's Kane, the guy I begged to help me, and he's done that, more than that really. He's fulfilled his part of the bargain and it's time to let him go.

I've just got to figure out how.

He's texted several times throughout the day, checking in and saying he'll see me tonight. I have to remind myself that I have to distance myself from him. My feelings for him are too complicated and taking things any further will only muddle things.

There's a faint smell of bleach lingering in the apartment from the nervous cleaning frenzy my anxiety had me doing. Charlie darts around the floor batting after a toy I just put back in his toy box and I thumb open my book searching for the receipt I used as a bookmark.

Right on cue, there's the familiar rumble of a certain motorcycle and I can't stop my heart from taking flight in my chest.

See, this right here is why I need to let him go. It's not healthy. He's helping me date, I'm not supposed to fall for him. Especially when there's no way he's falling for me.

We're friends.

Neighbors.

Nothing more.

It takes everything in me not to run over to the window and peek at him through the blinds. Boots clomp up the stairs and I can't help but smile knowing he's doing it to annoy me.

Charlie pauses his chase and freezes, cocking his head, his orange ears flicking as they pinpoint Kane's footsteps.

I glance over at the open kitchen curtains as he walks by. A dark curl has popped loose from his man bun making him look boyish and charming as he glances inside, his white teeth shining and grease on his hands when he waves giving me a crinkling wink.

And like a fool, I grin and wave back even when I know I shouldn't. Part of me wants him to barge right in here like he always does, pick me up and throw me on the bed and fuck me senseless like he did last night. The more sane part? That part tells me to cut it out and live with the memories because that's all I'm going to get.

Kane's lock clicks next door, the building rattling as he shuts his door. Through our thin shared wall, I hear water start to run and I try not to picture water running down his toned body as he showers.

Why am I doing this to myself?

Somehow I tune my focus back to my book—a more tame romance, nothing as risque as a why choose. It's not easy, but eventually, I fall into the love story enjoying the banter between the two characters, so I'm startled by the gentle knock at the door.

It can't be anyone but Kane. I'm surprised it's not the earthshaking pound he saves just for me.

My comfy plaid sleep shorts I put on after my shower ride up my thighs with each step and I'm grateful Kane can't see me awkwardly adjusting them as I step toward the door.

The door swings in, the air whooshing past my face blowing my bangs into my eyes. Kane's rumbling laugh tells me he saw the whole thing happen before warm fingers brush the hair out of my face.

"Hey, Else."

He's smiling down at me, but it doesn't distract me from the large duffle bag he has slung across his leather-clad chest. My eyebrows furrow as curiosity sets in.

"Hey. Are you going somewhere?"

His fingers fiddle with the strap adjusting his bag. "Yeah, actually. I wanted to stop by before I went in case you started to miss me." He shoots me a playful wink.

"Me? Miss you? You must have mistaken me for someone else."

Charlie shoots across the living room behind me, his claws scraping against the carpet. Kane leans around me, no doubt seeing Charlie run for cover.

"Clearly," he jokes. "I'm going to be gone for a couple of days. Ash's brother Garrett is fresh off the boat and we always hit up Vegas when he's free."

Disappointment settles in my chest at the same time as relief. Disappointment because although I pretend otherwise, I will miss him. Relief because this is what I need to happen to protect my heart.

"Ah, so a whole boys will be boys' weekend. I'm sure Ash is thrilled."

Kane chuckles, brushing a curl from his face. "He's downright giddy. Anyway, I wanted you to know."

I nod my head. "Whatever will I do without you?" I ask playfully.

"No one knows," he smiles warmly, teasing me right back.

His eyes twinkle in the fluorescent lights and I find myself looking at him a beat too long. Kane reaches for me, pulling me into the warmth of his hug. I love being in his arms, smelling the soap on his skin, and allowing myself a moment to breathe him in deeply. "I'll see you soon, Else." He pulls back slightly, ducking down and planting a sweet kiss on the top of my head before releasing me and walking away.

He's already down the stairs, his motorcycle rumbling before I suck in a steadying breath. "Bye, Kane."

• • • •

MUSIC BLARES THROUGH my apartment as I dance my poor drunken heart out.

After Kane left, I sat staring vacantly at the other end of my couch that Kane likes to flop onto feeling sorry for myself. Then I remembered the bottle of vodka chilling in my freezer for moments like this that Kelsey and I decided in college was a necessity. It's most decidedly needed tonight.

I may or may not have had too much, the music growing louder and my dance moves more uncoordinated than usual. Charlie has long since made a run for it, probably hiding out between the shower curtain and the shower liner like a goofball.

Winded and a bit woozy, I fall gracelessly onto the couch, the fort of pillows softening my landing. Pillows...and now I'm thinking about Kane and his creative use of my pillows that made me see stars.

God, I have to move on.

I spot my phone where I tossed it on the ottoman and lazily reach for it, not wanting to move from my spot, which took some gravity-defying moves, cheering when I grab it. I'm surprised I managed not to fall flat on my face.

Don't they say the best way to get on with your life is to try on someone new? Wait, that's not right. I scrunch my face in confusion, the popular phrase flitting away like a ribbon in the breeze.

Oh well.

It takes a matter of seconds, my thumb sliding over the glass screen of my phone and clicking on the dating app. The last time I looked through here was weeks ago with Kane who shot down every man on the screen.

Well, he's not here and I don't care if he'll approve.

A smiling man named Brad pops up on my screen. "Ooh, Brad. Let's see what you have to say." I scroll down further to read his profile. "Five foot ten. Pfft, yeah right, more like five foot eight. Likes baseball... Plays golf—kind of boring. Wants to salsa dance. Alright, Brad." With a flourish, I swipe right to move on to the next guy and take another swig of vodka.

This guy has me sitting up, the ground spinning as I do. He's handsome in a brooding way, with tattoos peeking from underneath his collar, blue eyes, and dark hair with a great beard. I push back the image of another tattooed handsome man. "Seth, tattoo artist, six foot one. Sold!" Swipe right.

Over and over, no matter what type of information I see on the screen, I swipe right. There's always some redeeming quality that I drunkenly give into. Because every guy I see on that screen? A deep familiar voice says 'Absolutely not' and that only makes me want to swipe harder.

Eventually, the app runs out of options with a screen popping up instructing me to come back later when they have more matches for me. Growling in frustration, I throw my phone and it lands on the floor with a dull thud.

# HEY, NEIGHBOR

The whole room is spinning and I groan covering my eyes with my arm. Blindly I reach for the remote and click off the TV, the apartment falling silent as I slip into oblivion.

A large, orange blob is tucked underneath my chin, claws gently scratching at the fabric of my sweatshirt. There's an incessant high-pitched ding ringing from across the room, the sound jabbing into my ears. I groan covering my eyes from the light sneaking in through the curtains gaining a mouthful of Charlie fur in the process.

Slowly I sit up from my place on the couch, one leg tingling from lack of circulation from where it hung over the edge. Charlie pushes off my chest with more strength than he should have, making me lose my balance.

Last night was clearly a mistake. There's a reason why I never drink this much, and how I'm feeling right now—like death warmed up—is exactly why. Cradling my head in my hands I breathe deeply fighting back a bout of nausea. Another damn ding goes off, the annoying and frustrating sound prompting me to stand on shaky legs.

It's not hard to find the phone face-down on the carpet close to the tiled entryway. Bending over without losing my balance or throwing up is a feat but I manage, unlocking the screen and muting the sound.

I'm about to toss it on the couch on my way to the bathroom, but curiosity has me unlocking it once more. The ding that so rudely woke me up isn't a normal text ding. Clicking on the notifications, I gasp.

How the hell do I have this many messages?

# Chapter Thirteen

*Kane*

Vegas with Garrett, who has wads of cash from his work on private yachts, is always a blast. Garrett's typically a stuck-up pain in the ass, but give him enough alcohol and his brother taunting him, he starts to loosen up.

Ash was beside himself when he got me to agree to go. Although the pull toward Elsie is unmistakable, it's clear Ash needed to let loose and I have been giving him the slip recently.

I feel like an asshole leaving Elsie like that though. She looked so goddamn cute with her bangs hanging in her eyes, her pink shorts creased from where she sat on the couch reading one of her dirty books.

Things seemed a bit stiff between us before I left, but I can't put my finger on what. I attribute it to us taking another step in our friendship. After all, it's not like I usually hang around after sleeping with a woman. But Elsie is different. I want to spend all the time I can with her, want to learn more about her, and want to feel her softness around me.

"What the hell, man?" Ash crashes into the bartop, Garrett close behind clutching his brother's shoulders. Both men have wide smiles and glossy eyes while I'm hunched over at the bar thinking about my neighbor. "Get off your ass and come play cards."

"I'm not one to say this, but Ash is right." Garrett rests an elbow on the bar and leans in next to his brother.

The two men could not be more different, but when they're drunk? Yeah, the resemblance is uncanny. He motions for the bartender and orders more drinks for us.

They're right. I've been off my game since we got here. I toss back the last of my drink and stand, clapping my hands. "Let's spend all Garrett's money."

Ash howls with laughter pointing to Garrett's shocked face. "That's more like it."

After several rounds of blackjack and many drinks later, I'm left to drag the Warren brothers back to our hotel room. Both men won and lost several rounds of blackjack, their hands never empty of drinks. I bowed out after a winning hand, not stupid enough to keep testing my luck and limiting my drinking. After all, one of us has to keep their head about them.

With a brother under each arm, we take up the entire hallway. Both men ricochet off the walls with dull thuds throwing off my balance. It's been a while since I had to take care of these two on a night out, but usually, I'm as drunk as the both of them.

Opening the door to our hotel room with two large drunk men is a battle. Garrett loses his balance and falls into the door as soon as it opens managing to catch himself before he smacks on the ground. Ash is no help clutching at his stomach with laughter barely staying upright with a hand on the wall.

I hook my arms under his and help lift him. "For fucks sake, Garrett." I'm lucky I'm able to get him up and to the couch, his big body bouncing on the cushions and sighing before passing out.

Ash stumbles through the doorway still chuckling, his eyes half closed. "Fucking lightweight."

"You're not looking too hot yourself." As the words leave my mouth, Ash stumbles again catching himself on the dresser.

"Still better than him," he mutters.

He doesn't object as I loop an arm around his waist supporting most of his weight and guiding him to one of the beds. Once he's safely on the bed I consider my job done. Ash slowly pulls his shoes off before flopping backward on the bed groaning when it bounces him more than he likes.

Ash falls silent as I lock up the room. Garrett snores softly from the couch. At least we didn't have to fight over who gets a bed like we usually do. There's no way I would've been able to drag his large ass to a bed.

The long day is finally catching up with me and I sink into the empty bed, my eyes drifting closed.

"You slept with her, didn't you?" Ash's voice is quiet in the darkness of the room.

I sigh, running a hand down my face. "Yeah. I did."

Fabric rustles as Ash climbs under the sheets, the bed creaking under his weight. Once he's settled, he lets out a long, drawn-out yawn. "Figures."

I let his statement hang in the air between us. It's none of his business what I do with Elsie. I try to keep the frustration out of my voice as I ask, "What do you mean?"

But all I get is silence.

• • • •

WE DROP GARRETT OFF at the airport before heading back home. He's off on another adventure in the glamorous world of super yachts.

Ash didn't bring up Elsie again and neither did I, even though she's constantly on my mind. Every several minutes I reach for my phone and check for a message from her, but there's nothing.

What's going on with me?

By the time Ash drops me off at the apartment, I'm practically bouncing with nervous, anxious energy. I've never been this wound up over a girl.

But they haven't been her.

I glance up to her window, soft light filtering through the curtains. She's never been good at being sneaky and I chuckle, waiting to see her try to covertly look down at me. But she doesn't. Disappointment settles in my gut before I remember that she has no idea I'm back.

Acting like a child, I stomp up the stairs, the soft rattle of the building acting as my welcome greeting. By the time I reach the top, she's standing on the landing with a hand on her cocked hip.

On reflex, a grin stretches across my face at the sight of her.

"You just had to rattle the entire building didn't you?"

I stop in front of her, looking down at the face I've missed for the weekend. "You needed to know I was here. Thought you'd like the heads up."

She softens, huffing lightly before turning to lead us to our apartments. "Hope you had fun on your weekend in Vegas."

"You know I did, Else."

She throws her hands up covering her ears. "Nope. I don't want to know. What happens in Vegas stays in Vegas."

Confusion flits across my face. All I did on my visit was drink, gamble, and wrangle two drunk brothers. She's the only person I thought about the entire time. Why would she think I took someone to my bed who wasn't her? The thought feels like sandpaper against my skin.

"Oh c'mon," I retort playing along, "I'd love to see you let your hair down in Vegas. I can see it now..."

"Shut up," she calls over her shoulder as I follow her into her apartment. "We both know that me letting my hair down is way different compared to whatever you're thinking." Her legs curl beneath her as she sits on the couch grabbing a pillow to hug against her chest.

My bag thumps against the floor and I sigh as I sit on her couch. "Hmmm," I hum in acknowledgment.

This isn't quite the welcome home I thought I'd get. Images of her on all fours as I bury my cock in her is more along the lines of what I was thinking. But I don't care what we're doing as long as I get to spend time with her.

Sex is preferred, but this is all I need. Time with my Else.

Quiet settles over us, but something keeps nagging at me. A subtle difference in the way she's seated across from me, not uncomfortable, but more stiff.

A weekend away after having just slept with her was a mistake. It's like we've taken two steps backward in the same span of days. Plus her comment earlier is interesting. I thought I made myself clear the other night.

I can't stop reaching for her with her being so close, finally in the same room. Calm settles through me with the touch of the soft skin on her ankle and I rub my thumb back and forth. "I missed you, Else."

She stiffens under my hand and I pause turning toward her. "So," she clears her throat, "I did some swiping and I have a couple of dates lined up. Your help is no longer needed. I'm cured," she says with jazz hands and a soft smile.

"Really? That's great." The encouraging tone is hard to keep up with. "A couple of dates, huh? I knew you'd be reeling 'em in soon enough."

As if listening to our conversation, her phone dings and she snatches it up fast as lightning. "I know what you're thinking, and no, you can't look. You have zero veto power."

I sit up, the hurt expression on my face not at all the act she thinks it is. "You want me to leave you to your own swiping devices? My veto reasons are valid."

"Ha-ha," she says sarcastically. "You've done your job." She reaches across and pats me on the chest. "You've been relieved of your duty."

"Fine," I hold my hands up in defeat.

She relaxes back on the couch and flicks on the TV. Her friendly chatter sounds muffled as she finds the next episode of our show. I'm confused about how we went from what happened the other night to this. Here I was, missing her and wanting to be with her only to come home to her ending our deal.

This was always the plan, right? I did my part—helped her build confidence and got her to come out of her shell. This was always going to be the end result. Now I can go back to long nights out and meeting new people.

So why do I feel so hollow?

# Chapter Fourteen

Kane doesn't seem upset that I'm ending our deal. It's not like I expected him to fight me on it—that's not who he is—but it confirms everything I've been feeling.

Part of me wishes he would've been upset though. Pride has a funny way of making you want things even when you know they aren't true.

Things went back to how they were before my feelings for him grew too much. Before the scales of our friendship became lopsided. He teased me about how often my phone chimes as we watched our current T.V. binge, but he respected the boundary I put up when I refused to give him my phone.

My once annoying neighbor has become my best friend, more than that really, but I can't lock him away because to do that would be to dim whatever it is he's sparked in me. He might not have romantic feelings for me like I do for him, but I need his teasing playfulness.

The man currently sitting across from me as he pays for our meal? Not so much.

Scott came across differently through our chats. He was nice enough in our messages, playful even, and I had no reservations about him when I agreed to a date. Now I've met him in person? It's a no from me. He seemed great on the app; funny, friendly, attractive... but he's less charming in person.

Maybe it's because he's not like a *specific* person, but I won't let myself think too much about that.

The warm breeze caresses my face sending my hair flying around me as Scott walks me to my car. "You're very pretty, but you look different in your photos. I wasn't expecting all this," he says, gesturing to my curves. Although his tone is pleasant, his observation isn't and I can feel myself grow smaller inside.

Kane would probably punch the guy for saying something like that to me.

I clutch my purse tight in my hands and try to quicken my steps. This date is over and I just want to get home and try to rally what confidence I have left. "Well, aren't you a wordsmith," I mumble.

Scott tries to save face, his hand resting between my shoulder blades as we step off the sidewalk and into the parking lot. "Don't get me wrong, you're attractive, I wouldn't have matched with you otherwise, but..."

"Oh I get it," I say, shrugging off his hand before turning to him with a forced smile on my face. "Thank you for dinner, it was nice, but I'm going to go ahead and end this here." Scott has the nerve to look offended, his face scrunching up as he holds out his hands as if to stop me, but I keep going. Standing tall I offer my hand. "It was nice to meet you, Scott. I appreciate your time, but we won't be doing this again."

He laughs ironically as he watches from where I left him in the parking lot. "Ha," he huffs, "you're doing me a favor."

I picture Kane cheering me on from the sidelines and smile to myself. Without turning back, I wave a hand and shout over my shoulder. "Bye, Scott."

By the time I reach the apartment complex, the summer sun has started to dip below the horizon painting the sky lovely shades of violet. Kane's motorcycle isn't in the parking lot and

I try to ignore the twinge that squeezes my chest at him not being here. He knows I had a date tonight, so he's probably out with Ash.

I want to share with him how everything went, how Scott told terrible jokes about how I'm a "cheap date" because I didn't order a dessert and offered to pay my half of the bill. I can picture the puff of Kane's chest slowly lowering when I tell him that Scott wouldn't let me pay. Can see his beaming smile when I tell him how I handled everything and how I stood up for myself.

A sense of loneliness hits me with each step towards home. The reality is that Kane isn't here. He won't be pounding on my door the second it closes. He won't be sitting on my couch listening to me recall my terrible date. No, he's out at the bar chatting up lovely blondes who have the confidence to approach him without their voice wavering.

Charlie meows at me as he hops off the couch in greeting. "Hey, bud. It's nice to see you." He purrs as I pick him up, cradling him to my chest and kissing his sweet little head. "Next time I go on a date, remind me that men are stupid." He meows once before flinging himself out of my arms and landing on his feet with a soft thump. "Great. Good talk."

Tonight seems like a disaster, but it's all for the best. Thanks to Kane's efforts, I'm able to hold a conversation and understand my worth. Scott just wasn't for me and it doesn't change how I view myself.

Showered and relaxed, I flop onto the couch book in hand. I've gone on several dates since the flood of messages started coming in, not all bad, but they all end like this: with me in my pj's cuddled under blankets on the couch with a romance novel.

It doesn't take long for Charlie to curl up on my chest, his orange fur tickling my nose as I fall into the story. My eyes begin to droop, the words blurring on the page, my glasses slipping down the bridge of my nose.

Charlie jolts upright, pushing off my chest and making me wince. "Ouch, Charlie. What the hell?" The book I fell asleep reading falls to the floor as I sit up rubbing the pain away. "Why would you do that?" I shout to his retreating rear-end as he dashes to a hiding spot which can only mean one thing.

Kane.

Why didn't I wake up to his motorcycle roaring and rattling the windows? Surely I wasn't sleeping that hard, right?

Heavy, sluggish steps clomp up the stairs, much slower than normal. Concerned, I push off the couch, the oversized shirt I'm wearing slipping down to mid-thigh, but I'm not worried about the amount of skin on show. Not with Kane, at least.

The night has chilled a bit with bugs bouncing off the overhead lights with tiny clinks. Kane's voice reaches the landing as he curses and laughs softly.

Wrapping my arms around myself to combat the chill brushing against my skin, I tiptoe to the concrete stairs lining the side of the building and watch as a drunken Kane leans against the railing, his chin resting against his chest as he chuckles.

"Have one too many tonight?"

"Maybe," he slurs, grinning up at me in that charming way of his, his dark curls popping loose and bouncing around his face. He sighs heavily and pushes himself up the steps toward me, his fist tight against the railing.

"Oh my God. Please stop before you hurt yourself." Rough concrete scrapes against my bare feet as I reach for him.

"Hmmm," he hums against my neck, his arm thrown across my shoulder as I hold him tight around his waist. "Were you up reading naughty books again, Else? I find that so sexy."

"Sure, big guy. Let's get you to bed." Together we take each step slowly, which is good because Kane is heavy and if he falls there's no way I'd be able to get him up. "Where's Ash?"

"Bike," he mutters as we step onto the landing.

"At least you didn't drive," I huff.

We finally reach his door and I leave him leaning against the wall as I search his jacket pocket for his keys. "If you wanted to touch, all you have to do is ask."

"Don't flatter yourself. You're probably too drunk to get it up anyway."

Kane tilts his head back in laughter, his voice booming across the complex. "I'm never too drunk for you, babe."

I roll my eyes. "Sure, *babe*."

His apartment mirrors my own, yet it's plain, lacking the personality of the large man hanging off me. When we get to his bedroom, he flops on the mattress with a groan, his eyes slipping closed.

"I'm going to take your shoes off and leave you some water on the nightstand." He hums in response but doesn't say anything more. "And maybe a trash can or something just in case." He sighs heavily as I pull his boots off, momentarily debating whether I should undress him further. I push the thought aside. That's not a road I should go down, no matter how I feel about him.

119

His trash can is empty, thankfully, and I plant it next to his bed in case he needs it. I don't think he's able to stumble to the bathroom in his state. Must've been a good night out, nothing compared to mine.

With Kane passed out comfortably on his bed, I leave him to sleep quietly, closing his door behind me. A familiar motorcycle rumbles down the street before turning into the parking lot. I guess Ash is dropping Kane's motorcycle off.

Sure enough, Ash pulls off the helmet and swings his legs off the bike before placing it on the seat. His eyes flick up to me briefly before he reaches the steps. "Is he good?"

For the first time since I left my apartment, I wish I was wearing more clothing. I cross my arms, hugging myself tightly, and try to push away the feeling of being too exposed. "It took a minute, but he's passed out on his bed."

He seems to sigh in relief, "Thanks."

Unsure what to do, I gesture to the parking lot. "Do you need me to call you a cab or give you a ride back to the bar?"

He steps onto the landing and I take a step back. "No, I'm gonna crash on his couch and keep an eye on him. He's done it plenty of times for me."

I nod. There's no need for him to elaborate because that's exactly what Kane would do. We reach my door and I pause with my hand on the knob. "Well, have a good night."

"Wait," Ash says, his hands fiddling with keys.

Hair slips over my shoulder when I turn toward him. "Yeah?"

Ash turns his head and looks around the complex as if he's contemplating exactly what to say. "He won't admit it, not even to himself, but—" he pauses, running his hand down his face, "he has feelings for you. I've never seen him like this before, so just... be gentle."

My head shakes involuntarily at Ash's comment, my eyebrows furrowed in confusion. "He doesn't—"

Ash chuckles softly, shaking his head. Swinging the keys to Kane's motorcycle around his finger he walks away from me and to his friend's door silently slipping inside and leaving me to stare at the space he left.

# Chapter Fifteen

*Kane*

Giving Else the space she needs is harder than I thought it would be.

Sure, we still spend time together, but it's not like it was before. She's more guarded than she was when we first met. Yet in a way, there's a glowing spark within her that draws me to her even more.

I want to see that spark forever. I can't bear the thought of someone squashing it.

Stealing her.

It takes half a thought before the bottle brushes against my lips. Fuck, she looked so beautiful tonight.

Ash was dragging me out, once again, when I ran into her on the landing. She curled her long hair and her bangs, finally grown out, are long enough to brush her temples making her look sultry and effortless. And her black dress? It had my fists clenching to stop me from reaching out to haul her into my arms.

She's been dating for several weeks now, and in some way, I'm happy for her. It's what she wanted all those months ago and she's really doing it. But it doesn't mean I have to like it. From what little I'm able to drag from her, no one's warranted a second date.

Tonight she's out with Paul, the guy she met at the bar. I'm hoping like hell he doesn't bring her here, otherwise I can't promise that my jealousy won't take over.

I feel like a damn caveman with how possessive I've become of my neighbor. She's made it clear that we're just friends who had a one-time lapse in judgment.

But can it be a lapse when no mistakes were made?

"Here, man." Ash sets the shot glass on the table. "You look like you need it."

I sigh, scraping a hand down my face before picking up the amber-filled glass. "No shit." Ash watches me warily as I throw back the drink. I've been feeling his eyes on me since our Vegas trip and I can tell he's worried.

Hell, I'm worried about myself too.

"Anyone here catching your eye?"

Of course not. The only person who's managed to do that is a small, curvy neighbor who reads dirty books and makes my heart stutter with her smile.

I don't answer. There's no need.

Ash shakes his head in exasperation. "What the hell are you doing, Kane?"

"What?"

"I was hoping something would kick in behind that thick skull of yours, but I guess I'm going to have to spell it out for you. Stop being a pussy."

"Fuck you. I'm no pussy," I object.

"You sure as shit like acting like it." Ash leans closer. "Who are you trying to convince here? Because it sure as shit isn't me. A blind person could see that you're messed up over Elsie. So what are you doing here?"

"Jokes on you," I mutter while taking another sip of beer. "I'm not hiding anything."

"Yes, you are. From Elsie."

Ash doesn't know what the fuck he's talking about. "What do you care? You've never liked her, anyway."

"Are you fucking kidding me? It doesn't matter what I think about her. You're my best friend and clearly, you're beating yourself up over her. You're going off the deep end, man."

The chair scrapes viciously against the floor as I push myself out of it and grab my jacket. I'm here to drink, not talk about Elsie. I won't sit here and have her thrown in my face.

Without another word, Ash watches me leave.

• • • •

AN OUT-OF-PLACE SOUND has my eyes snapping open.

When I got home, annoyed at my situation, I plopped on the couch where I fell asleep. But something has woken me up.

Sitting up, I listen carefully.

A dull thud leaks through the wall I share with Elsie. It's not uncommon to hear noises through the wall though. My Else enjoys her dance parties, so I let out a calming breath before sinking back into the couch.

At least she's home safe.

That's all that matters.

The weight of the alcohol presses against me and my eyes slowly drift closed again with a smile thinking about her wild dance moves. Right at the edge of sleep, a sound I never want to hear has me bolting for the door.

Elsie. Screaming.

Before I reach the front door, there's a loud crash followed by the sound of breaking glass spurring me to move faster.

"Elsie!" My voice is laced with pure panic—something I never did even while taking enemy fire. Within moments I'm pounding against the solid metal door of Elsie's apartment, more scared than I've ever been.

"Charles," she hisses and my blood boils.

There's a man in her apartment and he's hurting her.

"Open the fucking door!"

Heavy footsteps clomp over to the door and I prepare myself to deck the fucking asshole who dared to hurt my Elsie.

The lock turns, the chain drags free, and the door creaks open within moments that feel like an eternity. I'm on the balls of my feet ready to do anything I have to to keep her safe.

Poised for the attack, my fist draws back ready.

Except it's not an asshole. It's Elsie, her hair in a mop on the top of her head, her cheeks flushed red, holding a large squirming orange ball of fluff. Instantly my fist drops, but I'm fully focused on the room behind her.

"Where is he?" I growl, pushing past her and into her apartment and checking every possible corner.

"What do you mean?" She smacks into my back as I stop in the middle of her bedroom—an angry meow followed by a hiss making me turn.

I examine her in the lamp light checking her for cuts and bruises. Gently I run my hands down her neck, over her shoulders, ignoring the angry cat fighting its way from her firm grasp. "Where's the man that hurt you? And don't you dare lie to me." Rage simmers under the surface ready to boil over to protect her.

Her adorable face scrunches, her large glasses slipping down the bridge of her nose. "What guy?"

"Else—"

"There's no one here. I promise." She reaches out a delicate hand pressing it against my pounding heart.

"You were screaming. There was a crash," I state the obvious trying to connect what I know with what she's said. She's fine. She's safe, standing before me whole and uninjured. "Who the fuck is Charles?"

She squints her brown eyes at me, her lips pressing together as she suppresses a smile. "Did you not see the overturned bookshelf in your mad dash inside? I was screaming at my damn cat because the little asshole went into a frenzy and knocked everything over. Charles is what I call him when he's in trouble."

"This isn't funny. You had a date—"

"That I left early," she interrupts. "And his name was Paul."

All the panic rushes from my body leaving me reeling. Relieved and dazed, I lower myself on the corner of her mattress.

"Kane, are you okay?" With a gentle thud, the cat I've barely seen finally wiggles his way from the cage of Elsie's arms dashing into the living room. She stands between my spread knees and I don't stop myself from reaching for her bare thighs.

I swallow hard. Feelings I've kept hidden from her, from myself, have my hands shaking.

I thought she was hurt.

I thought I was losing her.

Maybe this is what Ash was talking about.

"I love you," I whisper on an exhale letting the secret I've held onto free. Her hands pause on my shoulders. "Seeing you go on dates has been killing me."

Stunned silence settles around us.

Her brown eyes are wide and brimmed with tears. A strand of her long bangs fall in front of her glasses and I gently brush it back. Her voice is hushed and breathy, "What?"

"I think I fell in love with you when I caught you reading that dirty book of yours."

She rolls her eyes. "Can you please leave me alone about that?"

"Never," I smile, rising to my feet.

"You're my best friend, Else. You're all I think about. When I'm not with you, it's all I can do to stay sane until I see you again." I cup her head in my hands urging her to see the truth in my words. "It killed me when you broke off our deal, Else. I didn't want to lose the only person that's made me feel more than I've ever felt. And hearing you scream? My world stopped." Gently tilting her face up, I kiss her sweet lips.

She falls into me, her arms linking around my waist as the kiss grows deeper. She fits like a glove pressed against me and contentment settles in my chest.

She pulls away slowly, her face flushed. "I never thought you'd have the same feelings," she admits, burying her face in my chest. "Never let myself think about it because it would be too painful if you didn't want me like I want you."

"Are you fucking crazy?" I huff sitting back down on the bed.

She sniffles, chuckling as she swipes at her cheeks. "Apparently."

I pull her to me, wrapping my arms around her waist. "I told you that night how much I wanted you. I meant every word."

"Well, I know that now," she says ironically. Her hands slide into my hair and I moan with how good it feels. "I thought you were just saying it to get in my pants."

"It worked, didn't it?" I tease with a smile earning a light smack on my shoulder. I pull out of her grip and gaze up at her. "I meant every word that night, Else. I've never wanted someone like I want you."

This time she kisses me, pulling my face to hers. "I love you too, by the way. I'm not sure when you went from my annoying neighbor to friend, to something new, but I know I don't want anyone else."

A mischievous smile stretches on my face. "Are you sure? I think George might want a second date. I'm sure he'd love to plant another kiss on these lips."

"Shut up, "Elsie groans and pushes into me. I drag her down with me loving the feeling of her body above mine.

"Only if you make a deal," I add, gripping her ass.

Elsie leans down, her lips hovering above mine. "And what deal is that?"

"That you're all mine and I'm yours. No one else. Deal?"

Her dazzling smile meets mine. "Deal."

# Epilogue

*Elsie*

This man is crushing me.

Kane crawls up my body kissing any exposed skin he can find. "Else," kiss, "it's time to wake up."

I groan at both his weight and the fact that I was sleeping perfectly fine in our bed until he interrupted me. "No. Five more minutes. You kept me up far too long last night."

Hot breath smooths over my skin. "I didn't hear any complaints." Cool air brushes over my nipples as Kane pulls the sheets low before sucking one into his mouth. Against my better judgment, my hands slide into his wild morning curls. "We have plans. Get up."

"What kind of plans?" I murmur, pressing a kiss against his lips.

He smiles against my lips. "Exciting ones. Now get that sweet ass out of bed. I'm going to feed Charlie." With one more quick kiss, Kane bounds out of the bed and down the hall.

He's bound and determined to have exciting things planned for us to do. In the last year, we've gone white water rafting, which scared the shit out of me, but what I found most interesting was the salsa dancing. Kane really knows how to move his hips, even if I stepped on all of his toes. So him dragging me out of bed after keeping me up all night is nothing new.

I just wish he would've let me sleep in a bit more.

"Is the sun even up yet?" I call down the hall to the sound of kibble hitting the bowl. Charlie's still not all that thrilled when it comes to Kane. I laugh thinking about the night he thought my cat was a man. I don't blame him for not knowing. Charlie still hides any chance he can get, especially when he hears Kane coming. He'll come around eventually. It's not like he has a choice because Kane isn't going anywhere.

Kane's voice booms from the kitchen. "Just hurry up, Else. And wear sneakers."

We moved into the small, two-bedroom starter home a month ago and boxes still line the walls. We haven't had the chance to decorate it yet, but Kane's looking forward to it. I thought it'd be me doing most of the shopping, but he's the one constantly sending me pictures of furniture.

I scramble to get dressed digging through boxes of clothes but not finding anything. He takes pity after chastising me with a playful smack to the ass and tosses me leggings, a crop top, and my tennis shoes.

A yawn sneaks its way out as Kane drives us to our destination. I can't deny that he looks damn good behind the wheel of the truck he borrowed from Ash. "You're still not telling me where we're going?"

Streetlights skim over his sexy, smug face. "You'll find out."

"Can we at least get some coffee? I don't think I'll survive without it. Are coffee shops even open this early?"

He squeezes my thigh. "You'll get your coffee. We have to do something first. Just wait."

With a sigh, I wiggle back into the seat. "Fine."

Gravel crunches beneath the tires before we slowly come to a stop. I must've been tired because drool pools in the corner of my mouth and I quickly wipe it away before Kane can notice.

I'm not sure how long we drove as I dozed in the passenger seat, but we're parked at the bottom of a hiking trail.

"Time to go, sleepyhead." Kane gives me a dazzling smile, looking wide awake and ready to go after our late night and early morning. He waits for me at the trailhead offering his warm hand as we begin our hike.

It's quiet and peaceful, if not a bit chilly and I hug my jacket closed as I rest my head on Kane's shoulder. Dense trees line either side of the trail, but I cling tight to Kane knowing I'm safe with him. The gray glow of the coming dawn filters through the treetops, the sun not quite rising.

Our hike is slow and unrushed mainly because the dim light makes it difficult for me to see where I'm going. More than once Kane has to catch me before I fall.

"We're almost there. There's a lookout around the bend I want to show you."

The trail is an easy one, aside from the wayward branches my foot would get caught on. By the time we reach the outlook, I appreciate that I'm not panting from exhaustion.

"Oh, this is beautiful." I walk to the knee-high fence marking the edge of the cliff and gaze over the rolling hills to the golden glow of the rising sun.

Kane's arms wrap around my shoulders pulling me back against his chest. I lean into his warmth and sigh as he holds me while we watch the sunrise. He kisses the top of my head squeezing me tighter. "Thanks for coming with me, Else."

I rub my hands along the forearms resting against my collarbones. "I love doing things with you. Just maybe not so early," I say playfully.

The sky transforms into an array of colors until the sun's rays cast a golden glow on us and the vivid colors fade away.

Kane kisses my neck before letting me go, the dirt shuffling under his feet. I take a deep breath, close my eyes, and enjoy the feel of the sun warming my skin before turning back to the trail only to stop short.

The man of my dreams gazes up at me from down on one knee. "I have a new deal to make."

My shocked face morphs into one of joy and I reach for him. "It looks like it."

"Else," he starts taking deep breaths to settle his nerves, "I never thought I'd meet my favorite person in the whole world when I moved into that shitty apartment. Never imagined the cranky woman next door who liked to sneak glares at me through her window would become my best friend," his voice breaks from emotion and he clears his throat. "I fall more in love with you every day. You've changed me completely and I want to spend the rest of my life with you. So," he sucks in a breath, "Else, will you marry me?" He unzips the opening to his pocket and pulls out a ring.

I throw myself into his arms, tears freely flowing from happiness. He's shaking against me and I hold him tighter before pulling back to kiss him. "Yes, I'll marry you." I kiss him solidly one more time, relishing the soft feeling of his lips against mine. "Wait," I pull back my eyebrows furrowing. "You knew I was watching you through the window?"

His laugh booms, echoing through the trees like a symphony meant only for me.

We walk down hand in hand, a new ring on my finger. Kane lifts our twined hands, kissing my knuckles.

Like him, I never imagined the love of my life would show up by moving in next door seeming hellbent on messing with my peace. But along the way, that annoying neighbor became my sense of peace.

My home.

Forever.

# Thanks For Reading

Thank you so much for reading *Hey, Neighbor*!

It's crazy the different things that can inspire a book, and let me tell you, there was a lot of inspiration for this one. Like Elsie, I too have an annoying neighbor who enjoys their loud motorcycle at all hours. Unfortunately for me, he's no Kane. Also like Elsie, if my neighbor looked like Kane, I would be too scared to talk to him too!

This story originally started as two different concepts that merged into one and I'm happy they did. I knew I wanted to write about an annoying neighbor with a motorcycle and a story about fake dating/ dating lessons story, so why not make it both?

If you read this story and were able to see parts of yourself within Elsie, then this story was for us, because who doesn't want their dream man to show up at their door?

If this is your first time reading my books and want more, check out my other series. Check out the completed Claiming Her Series[1] that follows the Williams siblings. Each book follows a sibling and their love connections.

If you're looking for small-town spicy romcoms, check out The Rose Prairie Series[2].

---

1. https://www.amazon.com/dp/
BOBJCM3QPR?binding=kindle_edition&ref_=ast_author_bsi

2. https://www.amazon.com/gp/product/
BOBS273PS2?ref_=dbs_p_pwh_rwt_anx_b_lnk&storeType=ebooks

Of course, you could always pick up *Yes, Captain*[3] if you're looking for a spicy, age-gap romance. Not to mention a familiar face might pop up...

If you could, please take a moment to rate and review on Amazon, Goodreads, Instagram, or wherever you post reviews. As an indie author, ratings and reviews are the best way of getting my work out there for other people to read. A little goes a long way!

Don't forget to follow me on Instagram @authorsierrashipley [4]and sign up for my newsletter[5] to get freebies and see more details about my coming books!

Thank you for your support!

Until next time,

Sierra

---

# About the Author

S ierra Shipley is a born and raised Midwest girl. She spends her days with her lovable rescue pup, Trip, who constantly wants all the cuddles. Her ideal day is spent drinking coffee, reading, and dreaming.

Sierra has always wanted the romance she's read in books. Pair that with an active imagination and a love of creativity, and you get a writer!

Sierra wants to create steamy, romantic stories with characters that people can relate to.